HAUNTED
OLD WEST

TwoDot/Globe Pequot Press Books by Matthew P. Mayo

Cowboys, Mountain Men & Grizzly Bears:
Fifty of the Grittiest Moments in the History of the Wild West

Bootleggers, Lobstermen & Lumberjacks:
Fifty of the Grittiest Moments in the History of Hardscrabble New England

Sourdoughs, Claim Jumpers & Dry Gulchers:
Fifty of the Grittiest Moments in the History of Frontier Prospecting

Haunted Old West

Maine Icons:
Fifty Classic Symbols of the Pine Tree State
(with Jennifer Smith-Mayo)

Vermont Icons:
Fifty Classic Symbols of the Green Mountain State
(with Jennifer Smith-Mayo)

New Hampshire Icons:
Fifty Classic Symbols of the Granite State
(with Jennifer Smith-Mayo)

HAUNTED OLD WEST

Phantom Cowboys, Spirit-Filled Saloons,
Mystical Mine Camps, and Spectral Indians

Matthew P. Mayo

Guilford, Connecticut

Copyright © 2012 by Morris Book Publishing, LLC

Text design: Sheryl P. Kober
Project editor: Meredith Dias
Layout: Sue Murray

Library of Congress Cataloging-in-Publication Data

Mayo, Matthew P.
  Haunted old West : phantom cowboys, spirit-filled saloons, mystical mine camps, and spectral Indians / Matthew P. Mayo.
     p. cm.
  ISBN 978-0-7627-7184-4
  1. Haunted places—West (U.S.) 2. Ghosts—West (U.S.) I. Title.
  BF1472.U6M3925 2012
  133.10978—dc23

                                      2012010767

Printed in the United States of America

10 9 8 7 6 5 4 3 2

*For my dear wife, Jennifer, the most spirited person I know!
And for Howard Hopkins, who loved a good ghost story.*

CONTENTS

Contents

INTRODUCTION

Before the Old West, there was the *old, old* West, a place inhabited for thousands of years by various native tribes. Spiritual residue, accumulated from their countless lifetimes, offers a filamentary foundation on which newer generations of spooks and spirits have since perched. We in the living world do our best to comprehend these curious entities, but despite our best intentions we still don't know much about the "other side." We have learned that some ghosts don't want to share their spaces, and yet others seem eager to let us know they are among us. Either way, that's when the inexplicable can happen, when we bump against the "spirit" world and have a genuine encounter with the paranormal.

In addition to our frequent forays out and about in the American West, my wife and I have had the good fortune to travel overseas. And it was on one such trip that we experienced the supernatural landscape firsthand. Several years ago, at the end of a long day spent touring in Northern Ireland, my wife and I pulled in at a massive old brick hospital-turned-hotel. That alone should have been sufficient warning that all might not be as it initially appeared. But the room price was right and we were "knackered" from riding all day, so we settled in. Before long we both knew something was wrong with the place, that our room was disturbed somehow; we just didn't know by what.

My wife and I spent a long, sleepless night filled with an uncharacteristic sense of genuine dread and foreboding. We also became convinced somehow that our situation was hopeless, that there was no remedy for our malaise. That heaviness pulled at us until we left the place early the next morning. Within miles we were happy (and relieved) travelers once again.

Did we hear any footsteps in the hall, see any strange orbs of light bouncing around the room, or feel the caress of spectral hands on our hair? Nope. But was the place, and our room, haunted? My response is an emphatic yes. I can only ask that you take my word for it. Was it interesting? In hindsight, absolutely. Would we ever stay there again? Not on your life.

Since then, though, I have become even more open to the idea that ghosts, spirits, spooks, and specters exist. Why shouldn't they? I'm reasonably confident that *I* exist, and I'm willing to bet good money that somewhere, a ghost may well be scratching his or her chin in indecision about me and my kind.

If we doubt too much, we run the risk of losing that sense of wonder, excitement, and raw belief in *possibility* we all had as kids. And that's too bad, because it seems to me we all want to know what we don't know. It's a basic human trait to flip over rocks, all the while suspecting we might awaken something that wished to be left alone. And that's good, because we like to be suitably shaken and stirred. If not, zombie movies would never get made.

Consider the grim scene of a pile of sun-bleached bones at the base of a mesa in a Southwest desert. Or the eerie silence of a ghost town long abandoned by the living. Or the sage-choked mouth of a mine shaft in a long-forgotten canyon. Or a lone, sagging windmill squeaking beside a tumble of logs, once home to a sodbuster. These scenes are all evocative of the Old West of both myth and history. And as we are about to find out, they are also ideal settings for the numerous specters, spirits, spooks, ghosts, shades, apparitions, hauntings, and other paranormal preponderance evident throughout the West of today but rooted in the slowly receding past.

Haunted Old West includes dozens of stories of some of the most actively haunted sites in the continental states west of the Mississippi River (plus Alaska). These locales are steeped in the mythos and mystique of the Old West, from battlefields and burial grounds to hotels, saloons, and wagon trails, from gold mines to ghost towns, from dusty Main Streets to swift-moving rivers, from ranches and cattle drives to stage stations and train tracks.

Not all the stories in *Haunted Old West* are ghoulish. Some are strange and inexplicable, some are touching and sad, and all are downright fantastic. Given the number of witnesses the attendant spirits continue to receive, it seems the stories are also true—at least to those who have experienced them, and that's good enough for me.

Just ask the tourists who've seen the agitated lone spirit stalking the ramparts of the Alamo, or the little lost boy led back to his hotel room by the kindly ghost of long-deceased Deadwood lawman Seth Bullock, or visitors to Big Nose Kate's Saloon in Tombstone, who share the bar with see-through cowboys sidling up for a shot of spirits. . . .

Where necessary, I have used authorial license to fabricate certain characters and combine various ghostly encounters to help illustrate situations and convey what at times is a considerable breadth of historical information in a limited number of words. All of the locations, accounts, and legends in this book are firmly rooted in the days of the Old West, most notably the era of bold westward expansion, and many continue to instigate ectoplasmic episodes and spectral encounters to this day.

Haunted Old West was a treat for me to research and write, and I hope it provides readers with a fun, enlightening entry into the field of paranormal writings about the spookier side of the Old West. It is my hope that not only will the tales in this book raise eyebrows, stiffen neck hairs, and quicken pulse rates as readers roam the pages, but also that they will induce readers to delve deeper on their own into the who, how, and why behind these intriguing tales, perhaps balanced on a log stump before the dancing flames of a campfire.

To that end, the book includes two useful appendices: "'Wanted' Posters" (aka the bibliography) offers ideas for further reading on the events and locations in the book—and beyond. "Saddle Up, Pard!" provides basic information for amateur ghost hunters with a curiosity for the creepy to set out on eerie Old West expeditions of their own to one of the many accessible haunted spots that dot the American West.

There's too much evidence showing that something rattles chains, clumps across the attic floor, moans in the orchard, slams the upstairs door, or screams in the basement to deny the possibility—no, make that the *probability*—that ghosts exist. And that's what this book is about: embracing the *probability* of haunted locales throughout the Old West.

I'll leave it up to readers to determine for themselves whether they believe. The best way I know of doing that is to visit some of the spooked spots mentioned in this book. You might go in a skeptic, but odds are great that you'll come out a believer. It has happened to too many people to think otherwise. (But you might want to bring along a trusted friend, one who doesn't scare easily.)

Happy haunting!

—Matthew P. Mayo
Winter 2012

Part One

WAGON TRAIL, EXPRESS STATION & TRAIN TRACK

Chapter 1
Dead Man's Canyon

Dead Man's Canyon
Highway 115, near Colorado Springs, Colorado

In 1863 homesteader William "Henry" Harkins built a profitable lumber mill near what would become Colorado Springs. He soon was savagely attacked by the Espinosa Brothers, Mexican religious fanatics. They cleaved his head with an ax, then shot him. Since then dozens of people have been chased by Harkins's ghost when they venture too close to the spot where his cabin stood on Little Fountain Creek. One woman even struck the spook with her handbag....

When he awoke on the morning of March 19, 1863, William "Henry" Harkins had no way of knowing that he would never again rise to greet the sun, or fell another tree and cut lumber to feed the sawmill he ran, tucked in the red rocks close by the bank of Little Fountain Creek, near modern-day Colorado Springs, Colorado. He'd come out west back in 1860 as part of a wagon train and, up until then, the only memorable thing most folks could recall his doing was saving the life of a five-year-old boy, little John McPherson, while on the emigrant trail heading West.

It seems the wee lad lost his footing and fell from his parents' wagon when it rose up and dropped off a rocky rut in the road, lurching its load, and depositing the unwitting youth on his head in the trail. Harkins happened to see this and shouted, "Whoa! Whoa there!" in just enough time to stop the wagon's steel-rimmed wheel from rolling right over the dazed lad.

In the following years, Harkins set himself up as the local sawyer and developed enough trade to keep body and soul together. He knew he could have an even brisker trade if he were a more sociable fellow, but he'd never been one for mixing with his neighbors. Other than occasional visits from people who needed lumber, he was left to his own devices, and that's the way he liked it.

But all that changed on that morning in March 1863. For that's when the Espinosa brothers rode up. He sized them up and labeled them as foul-smelling, ill-washed Mexican cutthroats from the moment he saw them. He'd heard they had been spotted in the area and now here they were, on his doorstep, killers and thieves nursing a secret anger over Mexican land lost to Americans.

Henry strode out of his cabin, pulling on his braces and squinting up at the brothers through the dappled sunlight as they rode up, bold as brass. They stared down at him, their begrimed teeth showing through split lips, their unwashed heads topped with drooping hat brims. "Hey, gringo pig. You got anything good to eat?"

As if in deep thought, Harkins rasped a callused hand across his stubbled jaw. "Well, now, let's see. For starters I got corn fritters fryin' up on the stove in the cabin yonder. And I got beans bubbling in a pot, and strong, hot coffee on there, too." He looked up, not quite smiling at the near-est man, then toward the other. "But not for any stinking animals like you, I don't."

With that, Harkins lunged between the two horses and made for his chopping block, where he'd sunk his short-handled ax but a short time before. If he could just make it to the ax, at least he would have a weapon. Give them Mexicans a lick or two before they did for him . . .

It took the two brothers but a moment to spin their mounts and give short chase. One of them knocked into him hard and ran Harkins down just short of the chopping block as the other leaped from his horse. Both of the men were shouting something that sounded to Harkins like a mix of laughter and rage. His vision swam and he saw the stamping feet of the two horses close by. He shook his head and tried to elbow his way out of that deadly dance.

As he struggled to his knees, then to his feet, he turned and heard a howling laugh, then someone shouted, "Stinking animal, eh?" Harkins saw a flash as one of the men lunged at him. *I'm done for,* he thought, even as he felt a sharp rap to his head and a hot flood of pain. He heard a strange guttural sound, didn't know if it was from him, and spun around in the midst of the little clearing. There was something in front of his face, like a big bee that wouldn't leave him alone. He tried to raise an arm to swat at it but couldn't seem to find the strength to do it.

All around him he heard a swirl of sounds, as if through water, the harsh barking of his hound, Samuel, the horses neighing, and all of it laced with laughter.

The Espinosa brothers howled with glee as they watched the living dead man lurch around the clearing, his own ax protruding from the front of his head, blood geysering up as if an overfilled wineskin had been punctured. This was truly one of the funniest things that had happened to them in a long time. That would help teach the whites not to steal land that belonged to Mexico.

The shorter of the Espinosas smiled at his brother, then drew his pistol, cocked back the hammer to the deadliest position of all, and fired but a man-length away. The bullet drove into Harkins's chest like a fist and he stiffened, his desperate hands clawing at nothing at all. Another bullet, from the taller brother, slammed into the man's chest, spinning him halfway around. They repeated this, then Harkins stiffened one last time; his bloodied eyes, whites bulging, rolled skyward, and a big red bubble rose from his mouth. It popped and he fell backward to the dirt and lay still.

"Ha ha! *Mi hermano,* look at that! He was a like a piñata, no? Now, that's hungry-making work. Let us see what that fool had in his house. All we wanted was a little food. He should not have been so insulting."

The dead man's dog skulked between them and the cabin, its yellow teeth bared and its ears lying flat against its head. One of the brothers drew his pistol and fired. The dog yelped once and flopped to the dirt, spilling its juices and spasming its legs as they stepped over it and into the cabin to eat. When they had finished, they rummaged the man's goods, and found a small stash of cash. Then they harnessed his only other possession, the dappled gray mare in his little corral at the side of the sawmill, and rode off, leaving Henry Harkins most decidedly dead . . . but hardly finished.

Shortly thereafter, the foul Espinosa brothers were tracked by a posse and run into foothills to the south, but not before they'd killed and robbed again. One of the brothers was captured and became the guest of honor at his own necktie party. The other escaped, fled south to Mexico, recruited a fifteen-year-old cousin, and returned north of the border to raid, rob, and kill for a time. Eventually they, too, were hunted down by an old frontier tracker and a small band of US Army soldiers.

The pursuers boxed the outlaws into a canyon and commenced to fire on them. But the young army men missed. The old tracker snatched up a rifle and dispatched the two scurvy killers with one shot each to the head. Then he hacked off those heads and carried them in a burlap sack to Fort Garland, where a fancy-dress dance was in full swing. The old-timer spilled the sack's contents onto the floor and said, "There's your Espinosas, by God."

Though avenged, for decades afterward Harkins's spirit was seen by a number of folks as he trod the paths of his canyon, sometimes accompanied by a white horse. And true to form, as he was in life, in death Harkins was a prickly pear. His continued presence close by his home and sawmill dictate the name by which the spot is known today: Dead Man's Canyon.

His spirit, complete with ax handle bobbing from his head, would often give chase to wayward travelers. Freighters whose routes required frequenting the region grew to cut wide tracks around the canyon, and still they were tormented by the grisly, grumpy specter for several miles. There seemed to be no predictable method to the ghost's menacing madness. Sometimes he pursued the hapless haulers, sometimes he merely glowered, his bloodied visage scowling from the roadside as they passed.

On one well-documented occasion, US Army Captain Marshall Felch was called upon by a young woman who was convinced that her fiancé, one Oliver Kimball, had come to harm in the gold fields of that region of Colorado. Felch arrived in Dead Man's Canyon near dark one night, and with the distinctive stench of putrefying flesh hanging heavy in the air, a white phantom horse thundered past him toward a cabin in a sad state of disrepair. Felch reined up and studied the situation, unsure what to do next.

Soon, from the cabin emerged an old man and a dog—both of them glowing and spiritual. The old man regarded Felch, then walked deeper into the canyon. It seemed to Felch that the man wore an odd headdress, or else something protruded from his head. Felch took a deep breath and followed. Soon, on the ground before him, he saw vaporous apparitions of two men struggling, then one man obviously dying. He looked up, but the old man and the dog were gone. The next morning, in full sunlight and with recruited assistance, Felch returned to the spot and found a fresh grave. The men dug it up and discovered Oliver Kimball's body, his partner's knife wedged to the hilt in his chest. (It was later found that the dead man's young lover, on whose behalf Felch was acting, had died at the same time her fiancé's body had been discovered.) Kimball's murderous partner, when tracked down and confronted by Felch, shot himself in the head.

This was apparently one of the rare instances in which Harkins's ghost behaved in a helpful manner. Numerous other instances of sightings and interactions with him were decidedly more frightening, one-sided affairs. On a number of occasions, the ghost was shot at by riders he attacked, but bullets had no effect and passed through his amorphous form. And yet somehow he was able to give chase, fling people from their horses, and bodily hurl them into the river.

But on at least one occasion, he was attacked by someone who refused to give in to his long-standing bullying ways. The person happened to be the indignant mother of a child he'd been frightening. The woman, in her haste to hustle herself and her offspring away from the angry ghost, swung her purse at the ax-headed Harkins and managed to connect with a parting shot.

Not content to rest in peace, William Harkins instead chose to rest in anger. Though since the late nineteenth century, sightings of him have been far fewer in number and frequency, they occasionally are still reported. It may be that Harkins finally came to terms with the fact that he had been wrongfully killed and that he was well and truly dead and would just have to . . . die with it. Or perhaps he is biding his unlimited time, waiting for just the right visitor to bedevil with his pent-up postmortem rage. It could also be that Harkins will make a righteous wrathful return at some point. After all, his remains were dug up in 1965 and moved a short distance away—to make room for a new road, Route 115, through his beloved stomping grounds.

Chapter 2

Beckoning Wraiths
of Cheyenne Pass

Cheyenne Pass
East of Laramie, Wyoming

*Late on a fall day in 1863, a wagonload of immigrants rolled into
Cheyenne Pass on their way to Idaho's gold mines. Their horses
trembled with terror and had to be whipped to move forward. In
the pass, Indian phantasms motioned to the travelers to stop. They
did not, and still more specters grabbed at them. They later learned
that the next party of emigrants was slaughtered in the pass. Perhaps they stopped. Today spectral Indians are still occasionally
spied there, beckoning to travelers.*

Barton reined up and turned back to Jim. "What's the
holdup?"

"It's them horses. They're acting like they're staked to
the ground. Can't get 'em to budge."

"Well, we'd better move them. It'll be nightfall soon and
I want to get on through that pass up ahead."

"What if they be Indians up yonder?"

This very thought had occurred to Barton, but he'd not
wanted to give voice to it. He lowered his voice. "Jim," he
said, lowering his eyes and looking at the man who was
as much a friend as a trusted hired hand. "You keep such
thoughts to yourself. It won't do to have the boys, and especially not Hilda and Lydia, hearing such things."

"I just want to be ready is all."

"As do I. We're nearly out of Indians in Missouri, least the ones that can make life miserable for us. We'll be better off on the far side of that pass, and not trapped here—or worse, in the middle of it—come dark. I say we move forward and don't nobody stop. Now help me roust this bunch. Pass the word to Yance. And Jim"—Barton looked again at his friend—"keep your sidearm ready and cradle that rifle as we ride, should it prove to be Indians."

He heeled his mount and headed back toward the wagon driven by his wife, Hilda. Beside her sat their youngest son, Reilly, and peeking out from behind was their daughter, the fair Lydia.

"Lay on the whip, Hilda!" Barton shouted to his wife.

"But Barton, the horses are frightened."

"Don't argue with me, woman. Lay on the whip and keep them moving steady, no stopping!" He spun his horse around and shouted the same to his older son, Yance, who rode at the back of the little train.

As he heeled his mount forward to lead the wagon on through, he wondered, not for the last time on this journey to Idaho's new gold fields, if it hadn't been a mistake to bring his family along. Maybe he should have just brought Yance and Jim, then, once he was established and making a bit of money, sent for the rest of his family.

"Too late," he muttered and shook his head to dispel the irksome doubts.

"What's that, Barton?"

He looked at Jim, who was closer than he thought. "Nothing, Jim. Let's just keep 'em moving. We'll be fine."

But the closer they drew to the curve where the pass opened up to reveal steep rocky rubble along either side, and the more he heard his wife snapping the buggy whip over the backs of the team—probably barely touching their backs, if he knew his wife—the more hollow the feeling in Barton's gut pulsed. And as they rounded the final curve that led into the heart of the pass, the hollow feeling crawled up his chest and clung to the inside of his throat.

There can be no good in this place, he suddenly thought. *No good at all, and yet I am leading my family and friend into this.* Even as he thought this, he realized that it was only going to get worse. The only sounds that came to him were the clumping of the horses' hooves, the rumbling creaks from the heavy wagon, and the occasional huff of labored breathing from one of the team.

His wife's whipping had stopped; the horses all seemed resigned to the fact that they must move forward, though a quick glance around him told him they were none too pleased with the notion. Their eyes were nearly rolled back wide and white, their mouths hung open as if on the first, raw edge of a scream, and yet they expelled nothing but near-silent huffing breaths and strings of spittle and foam.

The waning afternoon light grew darker, as if a huge bank of high-off clouds were settling in, yet Barton saw none in the clear sky far above. There! To his left, just ahead, moved more of a shadow than anything he could see. To his right, the same, a movement but not quite—and so it went, as he urged his horse forward, his rifle cradled in his arms crosswise, cocked and ready to swing should the need arise. And given these fleeting shadows, he was sure now that they had ridden smack into an Indian raid. He cursed himself, but he knew, too that the only way out was forward. This was a narrow pass and provided no room to turn the wagon. He prayed they would all make it through with their hair, with their lives.

He advanced, silently turning his head back behind him every few feet to check on the others. Always appearing just ahead of them, to either side, the fleeting shapes grew more distinct, and then he heard the whispers, feathery, snaky sounds that seemed to fill the air around them. But they were in a language he had never heard.

They hadn't gone all that far. Maybe they could go back. He turned in the saddle, but he was wrong; he saw they had indeed gone past the point where such an awkward maneuver would have been barely possible. He faced forward, catching Jim's eye as he did. The big man's broad face was sweating. He had never known Jim to show fear of anything back home on the farm in Missouri. Even that charging bull hadn't seemed to slow him down. But now he saw that his friend's eyes were wide, his mouth set in a grim line, and sweat pocked his face and dribbled down his cheeks.

They nodded to each other as they advanced deeper into the pass. The fleeting shapes became more distinct, tall and wavering like smoke rising straight up from the steep, rocky hillside to either side of the trail, growing like plants twelve feet tall. The whispers became moans that ended in drawn-out sighs.

But these sounds carried with them a veil of menace. The more he saw of these things, the more he realized that these were Indians, all right, but not the living kind. As he watched them appear, their mouths stretched like milky dough and sighs and moans came out. Suddenly it reminded Barton of something he hadn't thought of in years: the sound his grandfather had made when the old man had lain down on the kitchen table and his last long breath left his body.

Their hands waved at Barton and his people as if pushing at them, waving them back and away from here. "Go away! Go back!" they seemed to be saying.

No, by God, these were specters, the very ghostly souls of dead Indians come to haunt them. Barton was sure now that something bad had happened in this pass, and unless he could get his family through, something worse would soon happen. He wanted to shout to his family, to let them know that they must make haste, but he could not compel himself to break the near silence. It was as if the mounting gloom stifled his voice.

The most disturbing bit to Barton was that every time they drew close to the long, wavering specters, they disappeared, wisping to nothing, vapor-like, only to be replaced by others farther down the pass. This continued for two nerve-jangling miles as the travelers did their best to hasten through the defile.

As if by unspoken consent, the travelers continued their silence for long miles after they had left the confines of the gloomy pass. Eventually the frazzled party reached the Laramie River and did not stop that night until well after dark.

It was some days later that they heard of the fate of the very next party to follow them through the daunting pass. It seems that those people also failed to heed the repeated warnings of the wavering specters. But unlike Barton and his people, they did not make it through the pass alive and were slaughtered by, it was presumed, Indians.

"Timmy, you've never been more annoying than you are right now."

"Mom, Katy said I'm being annoying."

"That's because you are."

Carl turned to look at his wife. "Edna, that's a terrible thing to say to the boy."

His wife's face softened and she tucked her napkin under her paper plate. "I know. I'm sorry, Timmy." She smiled at the boy, so much like his father, spiked hair no matter how much comb wetting they did, and black-rimmed glasses they were each perpetually thumbing back up the bridge of their noses. "It's that book. I wish you wouldn't read it out loud while we're trying to have a picnic lunch at this nice road-side pulloff."

Timmy looked up from the page at his mother, grinning. "Why, Mom?" He squinted. "Are you getting scared?"

Her smile drooped. "Yes," she said, standing and scooping a stack of dirty plates and cups into the garbage bag. "I wish you'd bought a hat or an Indian-bead belt at that tourist trap. Anything but a book about ghosts. And especially that part you just read about the pass."

"Cheyenne Pass," said Timmy, locking his lips and preparing to reread it aloud, if only because his mother had brought it up. "According to my book, we're nearly there. And that's where those people were massacred, but by what, no one knows. They only found them dead."

"Timmy, please!"

"No, I want to hear it," Carl said. "Go on, son. What happened next?"

"Well, there's supposed to be a grave marker somewhere beyond the pass. It's where one of the victims is buried."

"Now that really is enough." Edna slammed the top of the cooler tight and headed for the back of the Country Squire station wagon.

"Tim"—his father patted the boy's head and winked—"I think that's enough for now."

The vacationing family piled back into the car and headed west toward Laramie City, though they were still some distance from it. As they drove, Edna wondered about the terrible things the white settlers had done to the Native Americans. *But really,* she thought, *did that give the Indians the right—even if they were ghosts—to massacre people as they traveled through? Oh, listen to me,* she thought as she looked out the window, *behaving as if those spooks in the story really did exist.* She looked up, smirking at herself, and caught her husband's eye. He winked at her and she knew she'd overreacted with Timmy.

And yet, as they entered the region of the pass, she felt certain that her husband drove faster than he needed to. And they all grew silent, even the constantly bickering kids. Silent and gloomy. Edna felt sure she'd never had a worse vacation. Everything about it seemed suddenly so awful. She tried not to look out the window—the last thing she wanted to see was an Indian's ghost beckoning to her, or worse, telling her to stay away, that a massacre was inevitable. . . .

"Carl," she managed to whisper as she grabbed her husband's arm. "Carl, for heaven's sake, drive faster."

For the first time that day, their son in the backseat didn't have a fresh comeback for his mother. Timmy was too busy staring slack-jawed out the window, trying to look away from the tall, wavering forms that seemed to blossom from the rocky hill beside the speeding car. Trying not to stare at the Indians who shook their heads and waved long, smokelike arms and shouted, *No, no, no, go back, go back.* . . .

Just before they made it through the pass, something felt as though it hit the car hard, as though a big rock had been hurled at it with great force. Timmy's sister screamed and bent low in her seat, her hands covering her head. His father swerved, the car squealed, and Timmy and his mother both stared out their respective windows at the shapes that looked with every step that drew them closer to the swerving car less and less like smoky figures and more and more like tall, thin Indians. Very angry Indians who moved with the speed only a specter could muster. As soon as the car slammed to a stop, half in the roadside ditch, Edna and her dear boy, Timmy, each scrabbled for the door handles, thinking that if they could just get out of the car, they might escape the wrathful wraiths. But the handles wouldn't open.

The family vacation was cut short, and any money Edna might have saved by packing their lunches was spent on months of therapy sessions for the entire family.

The region known as Cheyenne Pass, just to the east of modern-day Laramie City, has been the source of numerous reports of ghostly activity through the past century and a half. It began when white European immigrants began seeking their fortunes ever farther westward. Travelers claimed to have experienced spectral Indians offering confusing signals, at once menacing and warning travelers to turn back. Local newspapers such as the *Laramie City (Wyoming Territory) Daily Independent* and the *Torrington Telegram* ran remarkably similar accounts of travelers' inexplicable, frightening experiences there.

What caused all this terror and mayhem? Some of the people who witnessed such events lived to tell about them, and they all share eerie details about the mysterious smokelike forms darting from rock to rock, the apparitions that rise and fall, rise and fall from behind boulders and clumps of sage, always just ahead of the travelers, no matter the speed at which one's vehicle travels. Most agree that they were given warnings that helped them avoid potential doom. But it is the gold-seeking Missourian and his family who received the first and greatest documented gift—their lives. The following party was not so lucky. And now the single grave of a white man slain in that attack is the only witness still standing watch over the place so many are said to have seen the wavering Indian wraiths.

Chapter 3

Phantom Workers of Dove Creek Camp

Sinks of Dove Creek
Near Kelton, Utah

In May 1869, the completion of the Transcontinental Railroad linked the east with the west at Promontory Point, Utah, with a golden spike and celebrations. The Chinese laborers left the camps to work on other railroads or in the gold fields. More than a century has passed, and yet numerous visitors claim that at night, the ghosts of Chinese workers, their lanterns swinging and footsteps crunching, can be heard. And from out of the dark, spectral locomotives roar past.

Yun Li bent low, trying to block out the sound around him, trying not to think of the miles of track left to lay that day, nor of the vicious heat, nor of his dead friends. He looped the lift rope under the end of the oil-soaked railroad tie, and as he hefted the heavy timber, a single drop of sweat quivered, then dropped from the tip of his nose to the rough-hewn wood. The sweat and the quiet moment evaporated in the day's thick heat, and sound rushed back to him. He heard grunts and low moans, the steady yammer of voices, and above all the steady *ring ring ring* of hammer on steel.

As if reading his mind, the man he'd been working with for days now, a large, dark-skinned man who called himself

Noah, narrowed his white eyes and said in a low voice, "You keep your mind on the job and we'll both be better off."

"Yes, yes. I understand. It is just that I am thinking of my friend, Chin Lao." They placed the tie and immediately turned back for another. The big man didn't respond, but Yun Li, feeling more despondent by the minute, continued murmuring, unsure whether the big man to his left could hear him. It didn't really matter if he could, but to talk of Chin Lao did seem to ease the pangs of sadness in his heart. "He said he knew he would never leave this place. And he was right. Chin Lao was killed last night," he continued in barely more than a whisper. "That man with the shotgun, he work him to his death." He glanced up at the big man, who shot his eyes once toward Yun Li.

"Yeah, I know. You don't wanna end up like your friend, you keep your mouth closed. Time enough later for mourning the dead."

"You there!" A thin man with long, dirty hair and, despite the heat, wearing sweat-reeking buckskins, stalked toward them, a short, double-barreled shotgun held across his chest. "Keep your yellow mouth shut or I'll have your head roasting on a spit over an open fire, so help me God! You savvy?" He stopped just before the big black man and glared up at him. "You hear me, too, boy?"

Noah's jaw muscles bunched, one eye corner jounced and jumped, and his sweat-stippled forehead glistened. "Yes, suh, I hear you."

Both men bent back down, ready to heft another track tie, but the thin, stinking man stayed put, blocking Yun Li's path. "I don't much like your attitude, you dang coolie. I want some respect." He leaned down close and said, "Or you can damn well forget about getting time to bury your friend."

At that, Yun Li stood upright, his hands on his hips. "We must take care of our friend. It is only fair. He is gone. He depend on us." He motioned wide with both hands.

"I don't give a good yelp if you're responsible for all the buryin' taking place around here—and it's a lot; seems to me you Chinese ain't much of a hardy breed. But I'll tell you one thing, you don't get back to work and move double time for the rest of the day, you'll taste the lash. We aim to get this track laid all the way to the spot where them fancy fellers is coming to drive in the gold spikes come next week. And if you don't get the job done, you will find that I am a most unpleasant man." He leaned back and narrowed his eyes. A wide smirk split his stubbled face, revealing nubby, stained teeth. "Got me a notion to lop off a few more Chinese pigtails, just for the fun of it. What you think of that, Chinese boy?"

Yun Li lunged for the man, his wide straw hat falling backward off his head, sweat plastering his own filthy clothes to his lean body.

Up and down the rail line, workers stopped, most of them Chinese. Even the other foremen paused in their own duties and turned toward the commotion.

Noah thrust a big hand against Yun Li's chest, pitching the smaller man to the ground. "No," he said, pointing a finger at Yun Li. "That's what he wants." He leaned forward. "It's just what happened to your friend yesterday. I seen it all."

Behind him the thin, begrimed man in the buckskins roared with laughter. "You shoulda let him at me, boy! I'd have fixed his wagon for him!" He stalked off, still laughing, the shotgun draped across his shoulder. "Some other time . . ."

That night Yun Li, still mourning his friend's death, lay on his cot in his tent, dwelling on a feeling that he might never leave this desolate place. Too late, he heard the rustle of tent fabric behind him, then felt sharp, hot pain as something hard struck his head. He never felt the second blow.

Walter Tenzelmann woke up in his pup tent hearing a distant rhythmic ringing. Close by, several voices overlapped as if in contentious conversation. But it wasn't English they were speaking. It all came back to him then; it was the unspoken reason the group of eight of them, the core of students from Professor Whittlesly's parapsychology class, had decided to camp out here at the Sinks of Dove Creek.

He still heard the voices, and they were drawing nearer. A soft glow, too, crept up and flowered along the side of the little brown tent, filling the interior with a dull orange light. It must be a small flashlight, or maybe a lantern, and it accompanied the voices as whoever it was walked by. Walter was tempted to address them, but what if it wasn't Dewey and the others playing a trick on him? What if it really was the ghosts of the Chinese workers?

Walter eased the tent zipper up, but it sounded loud enough to wake the dead. *Wrong choice of words*, he thought with a wry smile. He hurried with his boots, poked his head out the zippered entrance, and felt the reassuring outline of his pocket flashlight in his coat pocket as he crouched low and walked around the tents.

A whispered voice said, "Walt! Hey, Walt!"

Walter froze.

"Up here."

He looked toward the voice and thought he could make out several shapes to his right. So that's where they were. He loped to them. "You guys," he said, low. "What gives?"

"Shhh. There are more coming. Look." It was Marcie, and she was pointing toward a waving light.

Walter heard the tape recorder's click and the slight hum of the little unit. Soon the voices drew near, but not just near the tents. They were all around them now, voices speaking in what was unmistakably Chinese. And they heard footsteps on the old rail bed as if made by many people, and random squeaks as though tin buckets or lantern bails were being swung. The students looked at one another, their eyes wide in the dark, each of them shivering, but not from the cold.

Despite his Germanic name, Walter was half Chinese, all American, and keenly interested in Chinese-American history. He had recently developed a deep interest in learning about how the Chinese were treated during the construction of the Transcontinental Railroad. And so he had been instrumental in getting together this group of friends for a spring-break road trip. The ghostly aspects were enough to interest half of them, but he, Dewey, and Marcie were the history majors of the bunch.

The sounds were from workers of the past, caught, as the professor had said, in a never-ending warp, a spiritual loop of labor, unable to leave this place where so many of them had worked so hard, had been abused, had given of themselves so fully for their job, where some had worked themselves to death. And so many of them never saw the glorious result of what the papers of the day had called "one of mankind's most monumental achievements."

Countless Chinese had died along the way, many of them right here near this longtime camp, the Sinks of Dove Creek, where the Chinese laborers lived in little stone, wood, and canvas shanties.

A far-off huffing, clashing, grating sound broke his reverie. All the young students glanced westward, toward the sound. For a second Walter thought he heard a train. But of course that would be utter nonsense. There was no train here. Hadn't been in the better part of a century, no chance of it at all since the tracks themselves had long been pulled up.

With the sounds of Chinese chatter still lulling them, from out of the far dark to the west, the students saw a pinpoint of light, its edges slowly fingering outward as it drew closer, and with it, the grinding sound increased. *There's no mistaking it now,* thought Walter.

"It's a train!" said Dewey as he scrambled to his feet. "And it's coming straight for us!"

Dewey, Marcie, and the others shouted and ran back toward the tents; a couple of them headed in the other direction. But Walter pulled his knees up tight to his chest, hugged them with his cold-reddened hands, and stared at the approaching light, surrounded by nothing more than empty nighttime sky for as far as he could see.

Dust billowed around it, and then a low, throaty whistle blew and the churning dust pushed ahead of it. Just as it reached Walter, tickling his nose, the sights and sounds and smells setting Walter's heart to thud like a drum in his chest, he heard a shout and felt two hands grab his coat by the shoulders and drag him backward.

He landed on his back next to Dewey and watched as whatever had come from out of the darkness thundered right where he had been sitting. The whoosh of rushing air from the unseen engine washed over them, ruffled their clothes, and kicked up even more dust.

Several minutes after it had passed and the dust had all but settled, Walter said, "That's one of those phantom trains the old-time engineers used to see back when the trains still ran through here. The professor told me that the engineers would be going along, then all of a sudden they'd see a train coming at them from out of nowhere. They'd hit the brakes, set up a squealing, spark-flying mess, but that train would keep coming. They'd stand in the cab of their locomotives and stare, eyes wide and jaws dropped as the other engine's light came straight at them—then passed right through them. *Through* them! Those engineers would scream as the phantom engines roared through, then they were gone, leaving nothing but wind and dust behind, their sounds and light fading."

"Whoa . . . ," said Dewey.

"Whoa, indeed."

For long minutes afterward, Walter and Dewey and the rest of the group sat still and listened to the silence of the Sinks of Dove Creek.

The Transcontinental Railroad's completion, marked by a ceremony in May 1869 at Promontory Point, Utah, was one of the most celebrated events in US history.

More than ten thousand Chinese laborers had been hired to help build the Transcontinental Railroad, and most of them toiled on the western leg of the line, working west to east. Their reputation preceded them: They were known for tolerance of punishing, dangerous working conditions that other ethnic groups routinely balked at. Chinese laborers on the western leg of the project laid ten miles of track in a single day—a feat unmatched by laboring groups on the eastern leg.

Once their efforts were no longer required, thousands of workers abandoned their homes at the Sinks of Dove Creek for the gold fields in Montana and Idaho. Only the occasional train ripping on through the vast, remote stretch of desert bore witness to the diminishing remnants of this once-bustling settlement. So many Chinese spent so much time there working, sleeping, eating, socializing, and dying that it seems the place was never really abandoned. It seems that many still reside there, though they are long dead.

Chapter 4

Ghost Rider of the Pony Express

Hollenberg Station State Historic Site
Hanover, Kansas

Hollenberg Station is the only Pony Express station still standing unaltered on its original site. Visitors who linger after sundown have reported hearing the sound of rapidly galloping hooves, then a young man's voice shouting, "Mail coming in!" Soon afterward the ghost of a Pony Express rider whisks by, appearing only as a blurred, hell-bent horse and rider, before quickly receding from sight. Some claim it's the ghost of one of the teenage Express riders attacked by Indians while trying to get the mail through.

Gerat Hollenberg had been dozing in the hardback chair by the fireplace. The only thing left of the heat-stacking blaze of earlier was now a layer of pulsing red coals. In his drowsy state he recognized that they were just right for broiling a potato. Not that he was hungry, for his wife had made another rib-sticking meal that the two of them had enjoyed hours earlier. They were alone in the station tonight, had been more frequently since the Pony Express service went belly-up months before.

He stared into the coals and contemplated scooting closer to them. It was growing colder. Winter would soon be here and the Kansas wind would resume its brisk-weather task of stripping away anything remotely protective, be it skin off a man's face, hair from a horse's back, or the flapping ears off a hound dog. Why did he stay here? Since the Pony Express had pulled up stakes, he was left trying to eke out a living by doing what he'd originally intended to do there: sell dry goods, implements, and other wares to farmers and westward travelers.

But that was a dicey pursuit even at the best of times—for as he knew only too well, farmers weren't the richest souls around. He sorely wished the Pony Express had lasted even a few years longer. No one had been more shocked and disappointed than he when the telegraph had cut off the Express at the knees and made it largely useless.

He missed those young, wiry men with adventure in their souls and fire in their eyes thundering up to the station, dismounting, knocking back a few dippers full of water, perhaps quickly attending to nature's call in the outhouse, snatching a snack from his wife's hands, and forking the next horse that would take them west or east to the next relay station, where they would do it all over again. These young men, brave to the last, were the embodiment of excitement and reminded Gerat of himself in his younger years.

He'd sailed to the United States in the 1840s from his native Germany and spent several years in search of gold in South America, Australia, and California. Eventually he amassed a small fortune with which he had hoped to set himself up in business, only to lose it all—and almost his life—in a shipwreck off the coast of Florida. He had spent months walking, impoverished and footsore, from Florida northward to Chicago. Once there, he rebuilt his fortune and moved to Kansas. And now here he was. Where had the time gone? And where had all those Pony Express riders drifted off to?

As if beckoned by his somber thoughts . . . that sound . . . it couldn't be—thundering hooves? But it was the middle of the night; perhaps it was one of his neighbors with an emergency. Gerat rose from his chair, struck a match, and lit an oil lamp. When he held the lamp aloft and leaned out the door, he saw no one coming from either direction on the road out front. But he did hear the distinctive drumming of hooves drawing ever closer. Then a bold voice, but a dozen yards off, called, "Rider coming in!"

Gerat held up the lamp, squinting into the dark, the sounds of a horse breathing heavy coming to him, blowing as it ran. Closer now, almost on top of Gerat, he heard the steady *clop clop clop,* but whoever it was didn't sound as if he was slowing down any. And then a musky breeze fluttered Gerat's shirt and the sound began to recede, to his right, toward the west. And all he could do was stare into the dark, squinting at some spot far beyond the dim, honeyed light of his lamp, toward where the sound of hooves thundered away into the night.

For a long time that night, Gerat Hollenberg lay awake in bed, listening to his wife's soft snoring, wondering about what he'd heard. He finally convinced himself that it was someone in a rush who rode by just out of sight in the dark, anything but what he feared it might be. And for nearly a week he managed to believe this. With each passing night he slept a little better, and by the time a week had passed, he had nearly forgotten about the frightening episode.

But then it happened again and again. Soon it woke his wife, then several of the few travelers who were still going westward. They all stood in front of the long, low-line building, and with each passing instance the shouts of "Rider coming in!" became more distinctive, the sound soon accompanied by a wavery, smokelike vision that over time became more distinctly shaped as a horse, galloping hard, and a rider bent low, his hat brim pushed back against his forehead, occasionally glancing back, as if he were being pursued.

By now Gerat, his wife, and their increasing number of nighttime visitors knew this was no living being, but the hell-bent spirit of a Pony Express rider. But whose? Perhaps one who had met with misfortune on the job? Maybe that's why the spirit kept glancing over its shoulder. Could it be the ghost of Billy Tate, the fourteen-year-old rider who'd met with a band of Paiute Indians in Nevada? He'd been killed by them, Hollenberg had heard, but the brave lad had also taken seven of the savages with him. Or perhaps it was someone who'd ridden closer to Hollenberg's station. He supposed it didn't really matter; mostly he was grateful that it appeared to be a ghost who was in too much of a hurry to stop.

"It's the only Pony Express station still sited on its original location and is now a National Historic Landmark." Hugh paused in reading from the brochure and looked through the windshield at the long, low building from the parking lot, then over at his wife. She appeared to be more interested in her romance novel.

"Aren't you going to come in with me?"

She glanced up. "Sure, yeah. Let's go. It'll be dark soon and we don't want to miss out on all the excitement of the tour."

Hugh smirked as he climbed out of the car. He knew Gladys was being facetious, but he'd arranged for them to arrive later in the day on purpose, though he didn't share that reason with her. He wanted to be here when the sun went down, and for as long as he could remain after that— as long as Gladys could stand it, that is. She would probably get cranky and want to go to the hotel.

But he wanted to be here after dark because that was when the ghost rider was said to appear. Not every night, certainly, but he figured that since he was here, why not give it a go? Hugh patted his coat pocket for his digital camera. He had enough battery charge for a short video clip and a few stills. *Maybe,* he thought, *just maybe I'll get lucky*.

The tour was fascinating, as he knew it would be. The place, now managed by the Kansas State Historical Society, was in great condition. The visitor center with interactive displays was informative, not to mention the well-tended garden plot behind the original station, and knowledgeable staff eager to share what they knew about the place.

But his inquiries about the ghost stories' being true were met only with smirks and head shakes. "Old wives' tales, methinks," said one staff member. "You know how people get. Anything out of the ordinary and they immediately begin thinking there's some supernatural reason behind it."

That news had been disappointing to Hugh, but not enough to deter him from waiting it out, along with a few other folks who apparently also had the same idea. Five people had gathered, one of them a docent who had stayed behind to chat with Hugh, one of them Gladys, and a young couple, curious about the ghost only because they heard Hugh ask the gift shop cashier about it.

And an hour after dark, just when his wife's sighs had reached the point that they would soon be followed with declarations of the party being over, far-off steady punching sounds reached Hugh's ears. Then the others heard something.

"Mail coming in!" shouted the wavery voice, then there it was, silvery and misty, almost as if composed of a smoke cloud lit from within. But this cloud was in the definite shape of a rider, bent low on the back of a hard-galloping horse and moving at a rate of speed no flesh-and-blood mount could ever hope to achieve. They heard the heavy breathing, the hoofbeats pounding on the grassed plain, the shout the ghost offered one more time. . . . For a long time after the vision and sound faded, no one said a thing. The five people just stared into the dark after the ghostly rider. Then Gladys whispered, "Wow."

Though he built it in 1857 to serve what he hoped would be a lucrative and brisk trade for emigrant wagons rolling westward on the Oregon-California Trail, Gerat H. Hollenberg's five-room establishment was ideally sited to become a major nexus point for the newly formed Pony Express in 1860. The facility enjoyed the benefits of two reliable springs of fresh, clean water and outbuildings, including a sizable barn that served as a livery with sleeping quarters above. The Hollenberg family home also served as the local mercantile, tavern, hotel, and unofficial post office for any letters from home that might be waiting for emigrants stocking up before continuing their westward treks.

But the Pony Express was a short-lived experiment that ended up costing its founders, its backers, and those in supporting positions, such as Hollenberg, much money. Within eighteen months the parent company, Central Overland

California and Pikes Peak Express Company, lost roughly $200,000 of its $700,000 investment when it was unable to secure a counted-on government mail contract. By October 1861 bankruptcy was declared and within a few years, most of the 163 Pony Express stations had been burned or were abandoned and left to ruin. Today the sole exception is Hollenberg Station, the only Pony Express station that still stands in its unaltered state on its original site.

But in its heyday, Hollenberg's facility was one hopping locale. Travelers would stand aside and watch as the famed riders thundered into view, shouts of warning resounding from the station's attendants. A fresh mount was led out, saddled and ready; the rider had only to transfer the specially built *mochila* (the saddle overlay that included four rigid leather pouches for letters) and reposition it on the new horse's saddle before he was off again. There was often another Express rider sawing logs upstairs in the dormitory sleeping space.

Express riders surged in and out of the place with the regularity of an oiled machine. So much so, in fact, that one in particular appears to have become a sort of spiritual perpetual motion machine—thundering in, then out again, hauling his phantom letters, and risking his spirited scalp.

Also in Kansas, and well worth noting for its historic Old West ties, Fort Leavenworth is the oldest active army post west of the Mississippi River—and one of the most haunted. The most prominent and tragic tale is that of the ghost of Catherine Sutler, a pioneer woman whose family stopped there in 1880 on its way west. Her children never returned from a firewood-collecting foray, so she wandered the region for months looking for them, to no avail. She eventually caught pneumonia and died. Her apparition can be seen carrying a lantern, forever searching for her children among the tombstones of the national cemetery.

The ghost of famed Nez Perce Chief Joseph, incarcerated at the fort in 1877, has also been seen on the grounds. In addition, spiritual tea parties, faces in fireplaces, and even the ghost of Lieutenant Colonel George Custer and some of his dead comrades from Little Bighorn have been witnessed roving the property at Fort Leavenworth.

Chapter 5

Tragic Spirits of the Donner Party

Donner Memorial State Park
Truckee, California

In the winter of 1846–47, a group of eighty-seven men, women, and children emigrating westward to California, were trapped by early snows at Alder Creek and Truckee Lake in the Sierra Nevada mountain range. Their food supplies dwindled and the weak began to die. To survive, others of the party ate the flesh of their dead family members. A state park now commemorates the tragic sites. And each year numerous visitors hear odd noises, feel hands on their shoulders and in their hair, and see glowing orbs along park trails, and when they get home, they find images in their photos of thin, sad strangers in nineteenth-century clothing.

Levinah Murphy looked at the emaciated sleeping children before her. They were too weak to do much more than sleep and, when awake, stare at her with hollow, tired eyes. Her own eyes were beyond tears. It had been so long since she had cried, truly cried. *But surely,* she thought, *with the death of children, I will cry.*

All around her people were dying, step by tiny step, their skin tightening over their bones, their breath coming in shorter pulls, the warm, hopeful light in their eyes slowly being replaced with a hardening of the heart. Long ago they had realized that all would not end well, and accepted the fact that death was the only certainty left to them.

She struggled out the door of the cabin, taking what care she could to not wake the children, and made her way, slowly, painfully, in the cold and foul snow, so much snow—deep enough for four or five men standing on one another's heads—and made her way to the long form out back. The half-wrapped, prone body was covered with another dusting of snow. She lifted the layer of rags and stared for a moment at the unreal sight of frozen meat on bone. Then she closed her eyes, breathed deeply, and set to the task, working as swiftly as she was able, hoping to get back inside and boil the meat on the meager cook fire before her children could see what it was she was feeding them. This unholy sustenance was her only hope that they might yet live through this hell.

On her way back around the cabin, she stopped and stared out across the frozen white expanse of Truckee Lake. What she wouldn't give to fly up, up and over it, to see it from above, then to fly onward, over the impossible mountain passes to the warmth and splendor that surely awaited them on the other side. She closed her eyes and turned her face toward the cold sun, a small smile succumbing to the bitter truth even before it had begun to grow on her thin, frostbitten face.

Larry Stein smiled as he thumbed through the photos he had taken on his recent trip to Donner Memorial State Park. There was beautiful, sparkling Donner Lake (formerly known as Truckee Lake), and there, the pretty path winding beside it. But . . . what was that off to one side in the photo? He leaned closer. . . . Yes, it was a little girl in a dress, staring out from the picture at him. And she had the saddest eyes. But that was impossible. He'd been alone on that path, he was sure of it. He would bet money on it, in fact, and Lord knew there wasn't much of that to go around. Especially on a schoolteacher's salary.

He looked closer at the picture, at that little girl, barely in the frame. There was something about her—something odd, aside from her sad look. She looked drawn out, somehow, thin and wan, not all there, almost like a . . . ghost.

Oh man, thought Larry, looking at the picture again. *Now this is nuts.* She was just some kid playing tricks on him. Probably did it to all the tourists.

But he couldn't shake the memory of something he'd read months before, when he was planning his trip. The spot where the Donner party had been forced to wait out the winter was said to be haunted. He remembered he'd laughed about it with his friend, Brian, as they had a beer after school. But Brian had told him to not be so hasty in his judgments. Wasn't he a schoolteacher, after all? And didn't that mean he should have an open mind? What if there really was something to it? What if ghosts of the Donner party existed? Who are we, his friend had persisted, to think we know all? Larry had had to admit that the idea of seeing ghosts of long-dead, cannibalistic pioneers had been intriguing.

But oddly enough, during the entire trip, he'd not thought once of ghosts, or ghouls, or spirits, or phantoms, and especially not at Donner Lake. But now here was this photo, sitting flat on the table in front of him. And staring straight at him from its square depths was a hazy-looking girl, as if the sun had bleached the image in that one spot.

The girl stood by the path he'd walked. He remembered now that he'd been alone, most definitely. He half wished he didn't remember so well. Then it would be possible that the girl could be another tourist.

He stared hard at the image and recalled the tragic history of the people for whom the place was named. Could it really be a ghost of someone in the Donner party? It was the place where they'd all spent that horrific winter of 1846–47, the one he'd read about on the plaque on the rock, and seen a program about on the History Channel. As he stared at the image a week after he was there and hundreds of miles south, inexplicably Larry's spine turned to ice and his face and hands went cold and clammy. For he suddenly knew, to the very depth of his soul, that he'd been alone on the trail that day. And he also knew, as he stared into those black-ringed, hollow eyes and saw all the sadness of the world there, that he was staring at the image of a ghost.

Larry nibbled his lip and glanced at the two other unopened packs of snapshots. It had been a great trip, but now he regretted taking so many at Donner Memorial State Park. What else would he find in the photos?

There had been that tall statue of members of the doomed party, looking forlorn and desperate. Something about the area had compelled him to snap away. The site of the Murphy cabin, a massive, flat-sided rock against which the cabin was built, had been another particularly affecting site. He recalled at the time feeling extreme empathy for the poor souls who had spent such a hellish winter there.

But now that he looked at the photos, Larry got the urge to scrutinize them far more than any other snapshots he'd taken on a weekend jaunt. Soon he sought more information on the Internet and read account after firsthand account of other people's odd encounters in the woods and surrounding locations, including at the Graves cabin site, less than a mile from the Murphy cabin site. Several people said that at the Graves site they felt as though someone had stroked their hair, then rested a light hand on their shoulders.

They had turned but saw no one, nothing out of the ordinary. Several had tried to convince themselves that it had been nothing more than a quick breeze, but now that they read other people's similar accounts, they felt as though they could overcome their fears, too, and share what they'd experienced.

As Larry read, he wondered just how those poor trapped travelers had managed to survive as they did. And then his thoughts turned to the ones who hadn't. The ones who were never allowed to leave that horrific place, the ones who seemed doomed to spend eternity roving the desolate spot where they died.

Even the slightest episodes of misfortune and woe in a person's life can sometimes be enough to doom the spirit to an eternity of wandering, confused, angry, and bereft of hope. Imagine dozens of people whose lives were drawn out in a most excruciating, slow death of exposure, starvation, and utter hopelessness. People who were forced to participate in cannibalism, half of them children.

And it all began in the spring of 1846, long months before starvation set in, back when the newly minted westward travelers first set out on what was supposed to have been a life-changing trip to the promised land of California. It was life-changing, but not in any ways they might have imagined. Eighty-seven people set off from Independence, Missouri, using a route recommended in a guidebook written by a man who never actually took that route. Following such dubious advice would be a major misstep on the Donner party's behalf. The most crucial mistake they made was in following Hasting's Cutoff, which ended up adding 150 miles to their trip.

This compressed their schedule to the point of danger, leaving them very little room for error should they slow down, become lost, and have to backtrack, or worse—all of which and more they experienced. From the start they had numerous other problems.

Many of the custom-built wagons proved far too heavy for their beasts of burden to pull. They were laden with furniture, built-in bunks, cookstoves, trunks filled with possessions, and more. Before the journey was through, the wagons would be abandoned and the animals would collapse from exhaustion and lack of water, starve to death, and eventually be eaten.

Before Christmas of 1846, two groups of intrepid souls from the full party tried to ascend the pass, now known as Donner Pass, but between weakness and record snows— the region received twenty-two feet of snow that winter— most of the members of the early rescue parties failed, became lost, resorted to cannibalism, or starved to death in the mountains.

At the two camps, people boiled chunks of raw animal hides, toasted hunks of fur-covered hides, and finally resorted to cannibalism while waiting for faint hope that someone from one of the two parties that had departed to cross the mountains would make it back with help. But with each day that passed, that hope dwindled.

In the end, eighty-one members of the Donner party became trapped, and forty-eight survived. But the region surrounding their woe-begotten camp near Truckee Lake (renamed Donner Lake) has since become a place of discomfort and dread for a number of its twenty thousand annual visitors.

For years after the Donner party's ordeal, other overlanders camped at the same spots, oblivious to what had happened there. But not knowing didn't protect them from meeting the long-deceased ghosts of members of the Donner party. In recent years, visitors to these locations (now encompassed within 3,293-acre Donner Memorial State Park, established in 1928) feel chilled spots, and recording equipment has captured the distinctive sounds of a woman weeping, and arguing voices of men, women, and children.

The location of the Murphy cabin, near which were found human bones and the partially devoured remains of other less fortunate members, is now marked by a large stone, part of the family's fireplace. It also marks the spot where an inordinate amount of spiritual activity continues to well up.

Several tourists taking snapshots within the region have returned home to find faint images of unsmiling strangers dressed in old-time clothing in their family photos. A vacationing elementary schoolteacher, liking the pretty curve of the path through the tree-lined woods near Donner Lake, worked to photograph it in an artistic fashion. When he returned home, he noticed that the developed image contained more than he expected. Imagine his surprise at seeing a thin, unsmiling young girl peeking out from behind a trailside bush. He swears to this day that he was alone on that trail. And yet he wasn't.

Chapter 6
Bandit Ghoul of
Six Mile Canyon

Six Mile Canyon
Off Highway 341, east of Virginia City, Nevada

In 1859, after having no luck in the gold fields of California, Andrew Jackson "Big Jack" Davis headed to the booming Comstock Lode in Nevada Territory. Tired of working so hard as a miner, he established a stable in Gold Hill, and business was good. Soon he opened a bullion mill east of Virginia City in Six Mile Canyon. He became a respected local businessman . . . who harbored a grimy secret: He headed a bandit gang that robbed stagecoaches, trains, and bullion wagons. Caught, then jailed for five years, he got out and picked up where he left off—and was shot dead while robbing a stagecoach. But he still had to guard his buried loot in Six Mile Canyon.

"Jones, shut your mouth, will you?" Big Jack Davis turned to face the fidgeting, whining man to his left. "Have I let you down yet?"

Jones swallowed audibly but didn't answer.

"Well, have I?"

"No, Big Jack. No, that's a fact. You—"

"Then stop sniveling and get yourself ready. Only way this thing will fall apart is if you let it. 'Cause the rest of us are ready to roll, right?"

"Yes, Big Jack."

"Now pull on those kerchiefs, secure 'em tight, and tug them hats down low. Last thing we need is for anyone to recognize us." Davis eyed each of the four men in turn. "Good, good. Make sure the bottom's tucked into your shirt; keep everything but your eyes covered."

"Just in time," said one of the other men.

"Yes sir, here she comes." Davis nodded and the five men all watched from behind the scrub brush as the Central Pacific ground into view.

As the train steamed closer, black smoke billowing into the clear November sky, its sound grew louder until it felt to the men as if it were about to roll right over them. The ground vibrated and gravel on the slope beneath them rattled and slid. Just behind them flowed the Truckee River.

Big Jack shouted, "Now!" and three men scrambled up the sides of the rail bed and ran alongside the express car until they reached its head, then leapt aboard.

Two others swung aboard at the rear of the car and made quick work of the pin connecting the passenger cars to the front of the train. Within seconds the passenger cars were receding from view. A porter emerged from the foremost passenger car shaking his fist and shouting unintelligible words at them.

Just after climbing aboard, Davis had battered in the express car's door and braced the Wells Fargo messenger with a pair of cocked six-guns. The man stood frozen, locked into a pose of sheer terror as the gunman approached. His two comrades advanced to the engine and the two pin pullers worked their way forward through the express car from the rear door.

"Don't give us a fight, friend, or you're cooked. You got me?"

The Wells Fargo man nodded fast, eyes wide, sweat stippling his clean-shaven lip.

The big bandit chuckled and wagged his pistol at the safe. "Crack that egg, then. I ain't had breakfast and I'm hungry—for gold!" His chuckles continued all the while the sacks of silver and gold coins were loaded into larger sacks.

An hour later found them well away from the train, riding to put distance between themselves and the law that was sure to soon follow. They reined up, a cluster of chomping, pawing horses along the north bank of the Truckee. Big Jack tugged down his kerchief and ran a hand across his stubbled face. "Well, then, like we agreed, we'll divvy the coins. But wait out the hot period, men. I'm telling you, a heist this big is bound to stir up a wagonload of trouble. Best we don't have anything to do with it for a while. Pretend you don't even have the money."

"I am going to need some of it, Big Jack," said R. A. Jones. "I can't live on air and beans; Lord knows I've tried."

Davis sighed, looked at Jones, and wished he hadn't brought him in on the job.

In his blankets beside his near-dead campfire, in the dark, small hours of the cold morning of September 3, 1877, Big Jack Davis watched his breath curl up before him like smoke. He couldn't sleep, an unfortunate affliction that had stuck with him since prison. His jaw muscles bunched tightly together as his mind drifted back unbidden to that winter afternoon seven years before when he and the other four men in his outlaw band had been sentenced for the train heist.

"It is the finding of this court that you, Andrew Jackson Davis, be remanded to the custody of Nevada State Prison for a period no longer than ten years." The judge's gavel had rapped the worn wood surface and sounded like the loudest sound Big Jack had ever heard. His was the last of the sentences handed down. All the men drew time at the state prison.

In the courtroom Davis had swiveled his eyes over at R. A. Jones, who caught his steely gaze, then looked away, his face reddening. *Good,* thought Davis. *I hope you feel like the fool you are. Going on a spending spree in Reno, then squawking out a confession and your friends' names like a captured chicken when they questioned you.* Davis ground his teeth together. *Someday,* he thought. *Someday I just may snap that chicken's neck.*

He'd spent half of his ten-year sentence in that hellish place—serving only five years because he'd refused to participate in the big breakout the year after he arrived. He figured he'd just get caught again, so he'd stayed put. He'd also helped the warden with what information he could about the escapees. Singing like that gained him his freedom five years early, and he'd been out for two years already.

And now here he was just a few hours away from another stage job, maybe his last for a while. He'd heard there was to be a shipment of gold, something he would sorely like to have. He could almost feel it—nothing like the thick, dead weight of gold in a man's hands. . . .

And a few hours later, that's exactly what Big Jack Davis was up to when it all went wrong. They'd seen him before he expected them to, but only because they had two shotgun messengers on board the stage. He'd barely had time to scramble into the road before they opened up on him. Two of the devils! Curse the Wells Fargo men for drawing down on him.

The devils shot me in the back, he thought as he lay facedown in a dusty, sticky mess of his own making, gagging on the blood welling up his throat. They hadn't even thrown down the strongbox. *I will not feel the warm weight of gold in my hands today.*

But his last thought brought a smile to his face. *At least I still have my buried gold, hidden and safe in Six Mile Canyon, where no one will ever find it. Not if I can help it. . . .*

Nils Whitby grinned when he heard the promising, steady *blip blip blip* of his detector. He paused and slipped off his headphones and admired the scenery, a pretty little canyon just east of Virginia City. His wife had given him the metal detector at Christmas and it had since become the source of many fun weekend jaunts into the countryside. Today he happened to be alone, and he didn't mind it in the least. Not only was this good exercise, but it was relaxing, too. And in a state like Nevada, with its history of gold and silver mining—and more important, all the robberies of shipments of such coins—he could be out here for years before he grew bored.

He'd chosen Six Mile Canyon because of that article he'd read recently about an Old West outlaw named Big Jack Davis. Weren't they all named "Big" or "Black"? There had been enough facts and dates in the story to make it sound somewhat legitimate. And it was only a few hours east of their place, so he figured it would be worth the travel time to get there. His wife had pointed out that lots of other treasure hunters had already tried—and failed—to find Davis's cache of gold.

"But they aren't me," Nils had said, a little annoyed at her lack of adventure.

And now here he was, smack-dab in the middle of Six Mile Canyon, in the very heart of Big Jack Davis's old stomping grounds. Oh, there had been some silliness in the story about a ghost scaring off treasure hounds, but thankfully, he'd never been the sort to put credence in such stories. They were probably made up by local treasure seekers to keep people away from their own rich pickings.

Then the beeping in his headphones intensified and the green light on the top of his detector unit began to flash more steadily. Nils worked the unit evenly over the ground, slowly back and forth, narrowing the area, then pinpointing. . . .

The next sound he heard wasn't anything he'd ever coaxed from his detector. Nor was it a sound that Nils would ever forget. It was a howling screech as loud as a train wreck that seemed to slam him from all sides, as if an audible weight had dropped from the sky on him. It cut straight through the feeble beeps he'd been concentrating on.

Nils spun, dropped his metal detector, and ripped off his headphones. He shook as he looked about, his heart threatening to climb up his throat.

He saw nothing.

It was near midday and the sun rode high. Then a shadow darkened the sky directly over his head at the same time the hideous screech filled the air about him once again. Nils's own screams were no match for those that came out of the thing above him. It was a massive fluttering phantom, shaped like a man but wreathed in white flame.

It descended on him fast, arms spread and impossibly wide wings unfurling from its back and propelling the freakish thing downward. Nils tried to scramble backward, but he fell, landed on his back, and managed only to throw up his arms before the thing attacked.

A wave of nausea and instant cold washed over him and fear blossomed in him, making his heart pound harder. The only thought Nils Whitby could keep in his head was to run, flee this foul place, get away before all was lost. He looked skyward as he scrambled to his feet. The thing was still there, still screaming. He looked around—no one else in sight. And Nils ran.

As he did, he could tell the thing was gaining on him, for even though he was running faster than he had since his dismal attempt at trying out for the track team in high school decades before, the feeling of dread increased with each desperate step he took. It rose in his gorge and made him want to vomit. The only thing that stopped him from doing so was knowing that he had to keep running. Had to get to the car. If he could just make it to the car he could get the heck out of here and never, ever come back to Six Mile Canyon.

It attacked him twice more before he made it to the car. Each time Nils screamed louder, lamented longer, felt more depressed and remorseful than the time before, and still it kept coming. And Nils kept running and crying, his own screams drowned out by the constant howling shriek of the hellish winged white ghost of Big Jack Davis.

It wasn't until he was nearly home that Nils remembered he'd left his metal detector back at Six Mile Canyon. And he didn't care. He wasn't going back. And he would never again wear headphones.

Only in hindsight did local folks realize that Big Jack Davis's legitimate bullion mill was a front for his "after-hours" work of robbing trains, stagecoaches, and bullion wagons—outfits charged with the high-risk task of transporting coins and ingots of precious metals. Davis then used his bullion mill to melt down his stolen loot before selling the resultant bars of silver and gold. Ever cautious, he secretly buried most of his profits somewhere in Six Mile Canyon, lest his newfound wealth be discovered and questioned.

But something about his time in jail appears to have made Jack Davis a little less than his old careful self. He was released from Nevada State Prison in 1875, only five years into his ten-year sentence, on request from warden P. C. Hyman. This good fortune was a reward for Davis's information about the twenty-nine men who in 1871 had participated in what is now regarded as the largest prison break in the history of the Old West.

Despite this kindness afforded him, Davis soon returned to his old ways. On the morning of September 3, 1877, while trying to rob a stagecoach, he was shot in the back and killed by a Wells Fargo messenger guarding the strongbox.

It is rumored that at the time of his death Big Jack left thousands of dollars of silver and gold coins buried along the north bank of the Truckee River just west of Reno. Treasure hounds continue to search the banks of the Truckee and throughout Six Mile Canyon in hopes of turning up some of Big Jack Davis's various caches of ill-gotten loot.

Big Jack's body was buried back in 1877, but he—or rather, something reminiscent of him—has been seen numerous times since, always in his former home of Six Mile Canyon, east of Virginia City off Highway 341. His larger-than-life ghost rises into the air, shrieking and howling in a ghastly, indignant rage only a dead man can muster.

His bright white form flies into the air, great wings having sprouted from the gunshot wounds in his back, and he appears to gather himself as if for an onslaught. Then the greedy ghost descends with the speed of a locomotive, straight at hapless treasure hunters, sending them scurrying for home, empty-handed and screaming in fright, vowing to never return.

Part Two

MINE CAMP, BOOM TOWN & GRAVEYARD

Chapter 7
Ghoulish Garnet

Ghost Town of Garnet
Garnet, Montana

The once-thriving mine camp of Garnet, Montana, was established during the 1860s gold rush and soon was home to thousands. In summer visitors frequent this best-preserved ghost town in Montana, but when snow lays a thick blanket over the Rockies, Garnet comes alive once again. From within the Kelly Saloon can be heard raucous music, and the J. K. Wells Hotel hosts spirited parties as the blacksmith's ringing anvil punctuates the sounds of Garnet's busy 1880s street scene. Yes indeed, Garnet is truly a ghost town.

"Stiff Pete! Get on over here and give us a kiss, mister!"

The shuffling old-timer scooped up two shot glasses and slid the half-full whiskey bottle off the edge of the polished bar top of Kelly's Saloon, Pete's favorite of all lucky thirteen houses of drink in Garnet. When he turned around he saw Maylene standing there before him, as he knew he would, trying for all the world to look like a sultry young temptress and not the beaten-down old mining town dance-hall woman she was. But Pete never even saw her graying hair, oft-repaired dress, and the crow's feet at her eye corners. He saw a friendly face who would gladly help him celebrate the discovery of the decent, if meager, vein of gold ore he'd found at his modest diggings just southeast of town.

"Hello, May. You look a sight tonight." Stiff Pete, so named because he moved slowly and awkwardly, as if he were afflicted with crippling rheumatics—though to his knowledge he'd never been—hugged the woman and guided her to a small, wobbly table near a side window.

She nodded at his bottle. "That's the bonded stuff, Pete. You get lucky today at the diggins?"

"You might say that," he said, pouring her a generous measure and another for himself. "Not a lot by some folks' standards, of course, but enough to keep me in groceries and"—he winked at her—"women and whiskey . . . for a few more days."

"Why, Pete," said May, mock shock arching her painted eyebrows. "Whatever do you mean, sir?"

He squeezed her knee. Maylene screeched a long, loud giggle and the night was off to the races. Soon a couple dozen men and women streamed into the saloon, the piano player, old Cotton, working those keys like they were good-luck charms. The place thumped and shimmied and the more people who crowded in, the more festive the night became.

Just like most nights in Garnet, this went on and on until the wee hours came and went. Most every night saw similar activity somewhere in town. And for good reason: The place was jam-packed with mines all experiencing long hours and decent payoffs. And the sufficiently lubricated participants just knew these nights would go on forever.

Del Pierson had held the winter caretaker's position for three seasons now and even though it was just a couple of weeks past Christmas, he was already hoping to get the job the next year. This, despite the fact that almost since his first night on the job three years before, he'd been bombarded with ruckus from all manner of "folks" in the little mountain ghost town of Garnet. Despite the fact that he was the only one there. Oh yes, he remembered that first winter. . . . When the noises had begun, he'd never been so frightened in his life.

That first night he'd just about gotten his gear stowed and his fire in the woodstove was beginning to knock the cold out of the little cabin's corners. It was a cozy little place, if a bit drafty, one of the cabins in Garnet that the Bureau of Land Management had been spiffing up since the early 1970s. He'd just settled into an old straight-back chair when he was rousted by a few hard raps on the door.

Hard enough, he saw, that the door rattled on its hinges. He jumped to his feet. Someone must be in trouble to be out on such a snowy night. He swung the door inward and a blast of stinging crystals caught him full in the face. But that was all that greeted him—no wayward traveler. And there were no tracks in the drifting snow before the door, no shapes of people standing to either side on the cabin's little front porch.

"Hello? Hello there?" Del shouted into the blowy, snowy night. No response. He closed the door and settled himself again before the woodstove. A stray gust of wind must have rattled the door, though he secretly doubted this, since the door was solid and bolted tight in place in its frame.

And then it happened again. Then twice more, and all the while, Del's eyes grew wider. He recalled the half-chiding cautions he'd been given by the old hands familiar with Garnet in summer and winter, men who worked on the fire-control team. He thought their warnings were mostly bluster and joke. He'd only half listened and never once thought to take them seriously. Especially when they talked about how the town was still alive, filled with sounds of what it would have been like in its heyday. They'd mentioned hearing the creak and groan of wagon wheels and horses' hooves clopping up the hard-packed main street, of doors slamming and people shouting; at night the sounds multiplied, and rousing music and bawdy, lusty laughter would drift out into the open night air.

That first night Del got no sleep. He spent the entire night feeding his stove, checking that his thin curtains were drawn tight so that no one, no *thing* could look in on him. Toward dawn of his first night, Del finally fell asleep for a few quick hours in the little caretaker's cabin.

When he awoke, he opened the cabin door. It was a lovely sight—sunlight glinting off what looked like a dozen inches of crystalline snow, all the buildings of Garnet capped with fresh powder. He'd snowshoe today, perhaps up into the surrounding hills. But first a cup of coffee sounded mighty good—especially after such a long, strange night.

The pot had just begun to percolate when he heard a distant ringing sound like steel on steel. He had no idea what that might be. Someone was out there. *Boy,* he thought, slipping into his wool coat and ski hat, *for a dead-and-buried ghost town, this place sure is hopping.* He strapped on his snowshoes, slipped on his mittens, and swung on down the main street of Garnet. There were no tracks at all in the perfect scene before him, just gentle swells where the snow had drifted in the night's wind. And yet ahead of him he heard the ringing grow louder and louder as he approached the little cabin that had been Garnet's blacksmith's shop. He stopped before it.

A *clang clang clang* rang out with a regularity that was the unmistakable sound of a blacksmith's hammer on an anvil. Despite the sun on his head and neck, he felt a cold, prickly feeling that had nothing to do with the weather crawl up his backbone and curl itself around his throat, like a reptile's tail.

"Hey!" he shouted suddenly, trying something, anything to make the sound stop. And it worked for a minute, and then it resumed. And from behind him other sounds emerged, as if someone had just settled on a good station on the television and turned up the volume knob. As Del stood there in the middle of the street, snow lightly swirling, the only tracks were his own leading from his cabin. And yet all around him sounds of a nineteenth-century mining town had come to life. The creak and groan of wagon wheels, the blowing of horses, an occasional shout from some unseen person . . .

He enjoyed it even as he wondered how it could be happening. Surely there was some forthright reason. Perhaps it was the altitude—he was 5,800 feet up in the mountains, after all. Maybe there was something in the water, a residue of something dislodged long ago during all that blasting and drilling and digging, something that affected the water supply and made him hallucinate.

Or maybe it truly was what one of the summertime firefighters had said, the "spiritual residue" of the place during its heyday that had attached itself firmly to this place, something that would go on forever, long after the buildings had fallen in and turned to powder.

That had been three years before, and now, as Del settled into another winter night in his little caretaker's cabin in Garnet, dozing before the woodstove, he found comfort in the fact that the town's spirits would thrive long into the future.

As if on cue, far-off sounds reached him. For all of two seconds he was confused. Then he recognized it for what it was—his spirit friends. The piano music, pounding and emphatic, was punctuated with bursts of laughter and the occasional shriek of a woman. Still, it wouldn't do to be lazy. What if it was really vandals this time? Del pulled on his jeans over his long johns, then slipped into his coat. It sounded like someone was down there, vandals most likely, or drunks on snow machines. He slung his rifle over his shoulder and tucked his flashlight into his front coat pocket. The moonlight was bright enough that he didn't need it—and besides, he thought, he didn't want to tip off the scoundrels that he was onto them.

That night was clear and cold and bright with starlight and moonlight reflecting off the snow. But it wasn't reflecting off the windows of Kelly's Saloon, where light leaked through the boards covering the windows and out from under the door. But as he drew closer to the saloon, quiet as he was able, the sound and light winked out. When he shone his flashlight through the gaps in the boards, into the old saloon, he saw nothing but a dark, dust-filled space with fallen boards, puckered flooring, and random pieces of old junk.

"Just making sure," he said as he strode back toward the cabin. He smiled as a fresh round of boisterous piano notes rolled toward him on the stiff, chill winter air, despite the fact that nearly a century had passed since Garnet's lusty, bellowing populace had been there. Since then the town had spent much of that time sagging in on itself, falling into disrepair, giving up its scant treasures to vandals and looters, devoid of any living humans. But Del knew the town was hardly dead.

For a town not built to last any longer than it took for all the local gold to be picked clean, Garnet has endured for a century and a half with surprising resilience. By the mid-nineteenth century, the region surrounding what was to become the town of Garnet, at First Chance Gulch, thrummed with the activity of fifty surface mining operations. But once all placer gold (surface gold found by panning, and using rocker boxes and sluices) was found, miners moved on to other promising locales.

By 1895 new mining technology made it feasible to erect smelters and crushers closer to the locations where it was suspected precious ore resided. Dr. Armistead Mitchell set up a stamp mill for crushing local ore at the head of First Chance Gulch in 1895. The town of Garnet, initially called Mitchell, grew around the location.

Miners flooded back into the region, especially after a miner named Sam Ritchey struck a rich vein of ore nearby in his Nancy Hanks mine, which would eventually yield $300,000 in gold, nearly one-third of all gold extracted from Garnet's two dozen mines. Within two years the town was home to one thousand people, forty-one of whom were school-age children, plus there were four hotels, four stores, two barber shops, a school, a butcher shop, a doctor's office, thirteen saloons, and more.

By 1905 the boom times had thinned to a trickle, the gold became a warm memory, and the population dwindled to 150 souls. In 1912 fire raced through a number of buildings in the tiny town's commercial district, and World War I reduced the population to a handful, though F. A. Davey still operated his general store and the hotel still stood. Then, oddly enough, in 1934 gold prices doubled and miners once again moved into the abandoned buildings and resumed digging for ore. But the boom was short-lived.

World War II pulled people away again. In 1947 the town's last remaining citizen, Frank Davey, also died. Shortly thereafter, souvenir hunters looted the town of anything that wasn't nailed down, and a few things that were, including doors, windows, and the hotel's staircase. By 1970 the Bureau of Land Management realized the town needed to be preserved, or it would all eventually be lost to vandals and looters.

Today, the Bureau of Land Management manages the town's remaining thirty buildings, helped by the Garnet Preservation Association, a nonprofit volunteer group dedicated to keeping Garnet alive. And the long-ago citizens of Garnet do their best to keep Garnet a living ghost town.

Chapter 8
Tommyknockers of the Mamie R. Mine

Raven Hill
Cripple Creek, Colorado

The cries of a young boy in a newly dug shaft at Cripple Creek's Mamie R. Mine on Raven Hill were too much for Hank Bull to bear. He rushed down into it—and was crushed to death. All that fall of 1894, the miners heard the screams of children and the pattering of feet, and caught glimpses of small, elusive forms darting through tunnels. Freak accidents killed men, and their ghosts roamed the shafts. Soon the mine closed, as men refused to work in a mine plagued by the little men known to miners as Tommyknockers.

The men paused for a break in the dank gloom of the new tunnel. Far below them angled the newest tunnel in the Mamie R. Mine. They passed around the water jug and the last man drank, then stoppered it with a cork.

Winton Felts stood and stretched. "Well, I guess it's time to get back to work."

But Hank Bull, a big, ham-handed Texan, said, "Hush up a minute, will you?" Hank stood and cocked his head to the side, as if listening for a sound he may or may not have heard, his begrimed brows knitted together.

Help me, Hank Bull! Help me. . . .

They all stood still for a moment. Finally one man broke the silence. "Time to get back to work, gents."

"Hush up already, I tell you!"

Help, Hank. Oh God, don't let me die down here!

"Why? What do you hear?"

Hank turned to his fellow miners. "I tell you, I heard a child, a young boy maybe. He's calling to me, shouting my name." Hank's eyes were wide and impossibly white in the dark of the tunnel. "Don't any of you hear it? Why, that's a child down there, screaming and crying and carrying on. If you men are too frightened to help it, I ain't."

"Hank, you're hearing things, maybe echoes from another shaft close by."

Hank continued to look down the shaft, but no further sounds reached him. He'd just about convinced himself that Felts was right, when he heard it again, a desperate plea just short of a scream: *Haaaank! Help me, Hank! Don't leave me to die down here!*

"I tell you what, I can't take it no more!" With that, Hank Bull headed down the recently dug shaft.

Three of his fellow miners raced to bar his way. "No, Hank! That's still unshored! Don't be a fool, man!"

The big man stared at them as if they'd just asked him to grow flowers in the dank grime of the mine. "But that's a child down there, asking for me! I have to go!"

Ignoring his fellow miners' pleas, Hank pushed past them, bent low, and walked quickly down the shaft, arms out, fingertips brushing the rough rock of the shaft sides. The other men stood, silent, wondering just what it was Hank had heard. They knew him to be a sensible, dependable man not given to fancy flights.

Long minutes passed. They called to him but received no reply. Had he heard a child? Maybe he needed help.

A throaty, wailing scream sliced the close air of the tunnel, echoing up from the deepest recesses of the newly dug shaft, rising to the gathered men. They recognized it as Hank Bull's voice. But there were no intelligible words, just echoing screams of agony. Some of the men bolted forward into the mouth of the shaft to help their friend, but within seconds a clashing, tearing sound gave way to a sudden cave-in.

It took the rest of the day to get the trapped miners out of the Mamie R., and after long hours, a stalwart few managed to unearth Hank Bull's crushed, battered body, long dead, his bruised face pulled into a taut mask of sheer horror.

Later the men sat together at a nearby bar, discussing the day's sad events. It would not be the last time they did so.

"Answer me this," said Felts. "Why is it that Hank was the only one who heard the voice?"

"Maybe he was crazy. Or maybe there was something in the water." Even as he said it, Tintotti knew his argument was hollow. They'd all drunk from the same jug. Then he saw some of the men looking at him sheepishly. "Oh now, don't tell me you buy into that Cornish hokum about the Tommyknockers." He leaned closer to Felts. "You do, by God. You believe in that malarkey!"

"Them Cornishmen are all the same," said Tintotti. "Always spoutin' off about them evildoers. I can't figure it out, though. It's not like they're using the Tommyknockers as an excuse to get out of work, for I will say that the Cornishmen work hard for their supper. So why the stories about the little people? Just to get a rile out of us?" Tintotti winked at the group.

No one said anything.

"Right, then where are those Cornishmen now?" Felts nodded his head as if deciding something for them all.

"They left the mine, I tell you. Left the employ of the mine for work elsewhere."

"That's their choice, though, ain't it?"

"Yeah, and our crew's small now. I tell you, they know something we don't. We need more men but can't get them to work the Mamie R. And all because of the Tommyknockers, superstition or no."

Howard heard the bell ring three times and almost didn't pull up on the windlass to haul up whatever it was—man or ore. Many times lately he'd hauled the bucket up to the top only to find it empty, a devilish trick played too often. He would have blamed it on the other men down below, hijinks of some sort, but the men all swore they wouldn't do such a thing, especially with the windlass. It was their lifeline to the surface and they treated it and the man working it with respect.

They all knew what had caused the false alarms, but no one dared voice those concerns, especially not while they were underground. And especially not considering what they had all begun experiencing down there since Hank Bull was killed. None of them wanted to admit that it looked as though the Cornishmen were right about their superstitions.

Many of them felt as if they were being watched, and yet every time they spun around, all they caught sight of was a fleeting shadow at the edge of their vision, a shadow that seemed to disappear right into a damp, rocky wall. The men began to hear voices, whispered skittery voices, sometimes low and uneven, sometimes high in pitch like a child's, but never intelligible. Then they began to catch momentary glimpses of the figures they'd long suspected were there: short, two to three feet in height, thin and wiry and with two eyes like coals glowing red.

And then one day in November, with no warning, the windlass creaked and groaned and buckled. The transport bucket rocketed downward before slamming into the skull of a man named Peavey, sledging him to death. Inspection of the mechanism proved there was no malfunction.

Still the mine's owners raged about slow progress and the miners worked the tunnels, shoring up shafts and expanding others, digging ore and sending it to the surface. And all the while they were increasingly tormented by the mysterious little beings, creatures who grunted and snarled into their ears while they worked. When the workdays ended and the tired miners caught sight of the Tommyknockers, it was always in near dark, and the little devils were in obvious good spirits, jumping and dancing, ecstatic that the men were leaving their subterranean realm for the day.

Next the spirits of the two dead miners began appearing to the men. While the haggard, expressionless Hank Bull roamed the shafts of the Mamie R., the fellow who had been crushed would appear in the transport bucket being hoisted aloft, his bleeding, battered head peeking up over the rim. And when he stepped from the bucket, he would disappear.

On Christmas Eve the mine flooded and the remaining miners spent the next day emptying the mine of water, one hoisted bucket at a time. Without warning the windlass creaked, snapped, and blew apart. Great spools of rope whipped outward and one caught a man about the shoulders and tightened around his neck as the water-filled bucket dropped like a stone. In the time it takes to snap a finger, the hapless miner's head was pinched from atop his neck, his head whipping across the ground.

Within minutes on that gruesome Christmas Day, the miners cleared out of the place and quit their jobs at the Mamie R. on Raven Hill. The next month the mine closed for good. No one else dared to sign on to work for the mine—or enter the domain of the vengeful Tommyknockers.

Welsh, Irish, and Cornish men, many of them descended from long family lines of miners back in their home countries, brought with them unparalleled expertise in working underground. They also brought with them a knowledge of things that should not be, evil things lurking far below the surface of the earth, creatures bent on causing mischief, mayhem, and worse. They called these foul skittering creatures "Tommyknockers," and many of these miners were all too acquainted with the "knackers," yet they also needed the work that the mines afforded them.

Debate among the believers wavers between the existence of Tommyknockers as being American cousins of the Cornishmen's "knackers," and the vengeful sprites in the Mamie R. being aroused spirits of Native Americans, angered by the blatant greed of the newly arrived whites plundering their resting place for riches.

There are numerous stories of Tommyknockers throughout the West, but of the decidedly less angry variety. Numerous miners claim they were helped each day by kindly wee folk who located lost tools, helped with little chores, led them from becoming lost in a tangle of mazelike subterranean shafts, and warned them of imminent cave-ins. But the miners also admitted that the imps were also notorious for playing pranks—stealing tools, lunches, tapping shoulders, laughing at them, and more.

Curiously enough, the State of Colorado has no record of the existence of the Mamie R. Mine on Raven Hill in Cripple Creek. But only because the mine closed before official censuses began in the state in 1895. Raven Hill still exists, and the region is riddled with abandoned mines and long-forgotten shafts. It is possible that should someone accidentally wander down an old shaft and become lost, they might well hear the screams of children beckoning them, pleading for help. Or perhaps they'll hear a hissing sound, and turn to see a shadowy figure barely waist high, eyes glowing like hot coals, an impish grin on its face. The Tommyknocker might help guide them to the surface. Or not.

Chapter 9
Sinkpit of Sin
and Damnation

Ghost Town of Bodie, State Historic Park
Bodie, California

Kept in an official state of "arrested decay" (protected but not restored), Bodie, California, is one of America's best-preserved ghost towns. It's also one of its most haunted. Many of the 170-plus structures in town are occupied by ghosts, including the Cain house, in which a Chinese maid committed suicide. All over town, voices can be heard, and ghosts move objects and stare from windows. The Curse of Bodie says that anyone who removes an item from the town will experience misfortune until the item is returned. Each year park rangers receive looted items in the mail, with letters of apology to the spirits of Bodie.

"You got to go on home now, Evelyn. I appreciate you walking me to work, but your mama's going to be wondering where you are. And this weather's fixing to brew up a storm." Willard looked down at the little smiling girl. *Every day she follows me to work, makes sure I get here okay. It's flattering.*

As he watched little Evelyn turn and go, she looked back and smiled at him. He smiled and nodded. It was sure to be a stormy day and in Bodie it could get downright nasty, but she didn't live that far away, so he knew she would make it home before the weather turned.

Willard hefted his pick, wrapped his callused hands around the long, polished hardwood handle, and sighed. Another long day of busting rock. *Keep your eyes on the ore, Will,* he told himself. *Keep your mind focused on finding gold and you'll strike it rich before long.* Isn't that what the man at the saloon said just last week? That his company was moving in and setting up a crushing machine because they were so convinced that Bodie was sitting on one of the world's largest gold deposits ever seen. Just a matter of figuring out how to get it out of the ground.

And where there were companies willing to invest, there would be jobs for fellas like Willard. Grew up doing hard labor, so no reason to not keep on swinging a pick, busting rock for someone else. But only until he could afford his own claim. And Bodie, by God, was the place to do it. His thoughts flashed briefly on his little good-luck charm, as he called the little girl. He smiled as he raised the pick. With a lucky talisman like Evelyn, who needed anything else? He'd supply the labor; she'd supply the luck.

Willard swung the pick high and hard, way back behind himself, intending to make his first swing of the day a mighty one. But the pick struck something behind him. He spun . . . and in that flash of a second he knew his life would never be the same again. He'd struck the little girl square in the top of her head with the pick. She lay on her side, little arms flailing feebly, blood running from her mouth. But it was the eyes, Evelyn's dear little eyes staring at him. And he swore she was still smiling that sweet little innocent smile.

The townspeople did their best to comfort the grief-stricken miner, Evelyn's friend and also the unwitting killer of the innocent four-year-old. But he took it hard and never really recovered. A fancy headstone with a little angel on top was erected at the girl's grave. And then she began appearing to visitors, mostly in the cemetery, or rather her ghost did. And much to their surprise, hers was not a ghost angry at its plight.

The little girl's spirit form is as the girl had been—sweet, kindly, and smiling. To this day people report having seen the hazy, gauzy figure of the girl in various spots about the town, and most often on nights of the full moon, when the entire town is lit from above. They nod and quietly say, "Look, it's the Angel of Bodie." And the little Angel of Bodie will smile at them.

To Whom It May Concern:

Last year my family and I visited Bodie in July. We toured the town, the various buildings and homes. I can't say it was enjoyable. It was interesting, though. But the real reason I'm writing is because, and I am ashamed to admit it, and it's so embarrassing, but I really wanted something to remember this place by when I was back home in Waukesha, Wisconsin. So I took something from one of the houses—the J. S. Cain house, I believe. Really, it's just a small thing, a spoon from a drawer in the kitchen. But I realize now that I should not have done it. It's not like it was stealing, really, but, and I know this sounds silly, but since we came home and that spoon has been here, one bad thing after another has happened to my family.

I can't think of anything else that might be the cause, other than that spoon. I never should have taken it. That's why you'll find it enclosed in this package. I went online and found out that this has happened to lots of other people, too, so I put two and two together and came up with the idea of sending back the spoon to you.

If you would be so kind, please put it back in the kitchen drawer of the Cain house for me. And maybe please tell the ghosts there—because we were told that the place is really haunted—that I am really sorry and I hope that any distress I caused the spirits there in Bodie is okay now. Honestly, I can't think of anything else it might be. But our lives can't take much more of this Bodie bad luck.

Sincerely,
Wilma Huggins

Ranger Parker sighed, folded the letter, and stuffed it back into its envelope. He upended the small box the letter had come in, and out slid an old tarnished soup spoon—thin at the edges, and scratched and looking hardly worth the effort Wilma Huggins had invested in it. But Ranger Parker knew better. He put on his hat and stuffed the spoon into his pants pocket. *No time like the present,* he thought as he headed out the door of the ranger's office.

This made the fourth returned item this month, and it was only the 20th of June. When would people learn? They were told when they got here that the place was a state historic park preserved in a state of arrested decay. They were also told that they must not touch anything as they toured the wind-dried husk of a town. It was left this way intentionally, pretty much resembling a town that was abandoned just after breakfast but before the dishes were done. And in some instances, that truly seemed the case, so startling do some of the abodes appear. Clothes still on racks, dishes still stacked in dry sinks, cupboards still filled with possessions.

But visitors become so fascinated with the place that they think they need a keepsake of their time touring it. And since they see all those things owned by former occupants of the desolate town, they think that one little item won't be missed, surely. And while a ranger might not miss it, over time if everyone did it, the town would be stripped bare. But more to the point, the ghosts missed those items. It was as if they were always watching. And from what Ranger Parker knew firsthand, there were plenty of ghosts in Bodie, enough to give the term "ghost town" a whole different meaning.

He whistled as he walked to the J. S. Cain house. In his pocket, he wrapped his fingers around the shaft of the old, bowed spoon. As soon as he slid the drawer out a bit and slipped the spoon inside, he paused to listen, and could swear he heard a barely audible sigh, as if the very meager act of replacing the long-lost spoon caused someone immeasurable relief.

"Well," he said to the still room, "I hope that satisfies you now. Mrs. Huggins seems like an awfully nice lady who really didn't mean to cause anybody harm here. She must have really liked the place, enough to want to remember it from afar. So if you're happy again, maybe you could make it so her life isn't affected by whatever it is she feels has been troubling her and her family."

Ranger Parker stood like that for a moment in the empty room, then smiled and nodded at no one—no one he could see, that is. He knew he didn't have to do it, but he knew the ghosts existed and there had been enough instances

that he figured he should attend to these matters personally, just in case. He continued on outside and pulled his hat
brim down tight against the double assault of the glaring
sun and the stinging dust.

As he made his way back to his office he wondered how
many more packages he would receive before the month was
up, from people desperate to rid themselves of the horrible
bad luck that had become their lot since they had stolen a
seemingly insignificant item from Bodie, a keepsake that
had turned their lives into living nightmares.

The history of Bodie is one of economic ups and downs.
Indeed, the boom-bust-boom-bust aspect of Bodie's history
is one of its most striking traits. Gold was first discovered
there in 1859, but a freak mine cave-in in 1875 led to Bodie's first big boom period, as previously unseen gold deposits
were discovered when the rubble was cleared away. Other
chance, uncontrollable episodes were not so fortunate for
the people of Bodie. Shortly after the boom period began,
the unforgiving winter of 1878–1879 wiped out hundreds
due to exposure, frostbite, and rampant disease. Numerous
accidents including mine cave-ins, uncontrolled explosions,
fires, and more all took their toll on the town, which seemed
always to have more than its share of bad luck.

Despite this, by 1880 Bodie was home to ten thousand
people and roughly eight hundred buildings, including
saloons, churches, brothels, markets, schools, and more. So
rambunctious and lawless was the general populace of Bodie
that at various times the town was called "a sinkpit of sin
and damnation" and "the most godforsaken place on earth."

It is said that one young girl, on the eve of her family's move from San Francisco to Bodie, wrote in her diary, "Goodbye God, I'm going to Bodie." Though another interpretation claims she wrote, "Good, by God, I'm going to Bodie," which seems the less likely of the two, given that Bodie at the time was a largely lawless place rife with rough people engaged in working hard, and playing harder.

Its decline took more than a half century, and by the mid-1950s the last of the meager gold pickings had been extracted using a method involving cyanide. The few remaining residents had next to nothing, and loaded what they could carry onto their family conveyance—car or horse-drawn wagon—and left the rest where it lay in their homes and yards. And those possessions can be seen today, watched over by the ghosts of the thousands of souls who still call Bodie home. Judging from the large number of ghosts and haunted buildings in Bodie, it is likely that all that rough living left a large amount of spiritual residue that seems to suit ghosts just fine. After all, they seem in no hurry to move on.

Chapter 10
Boot Hill and Beyond

Boot Hill Cemetery
Idaho City, Idaho

Established in 1862 when gold was struck in the nearby hills and valleys of Boise Basin, the town saw its population bubble to thousands, with hundreds of businesses. Today Boot Hill and Pioneer Cemeteries are populated with a good many ghosts: A young Chinese girl weeps over a grave, and an old prospector in Western garb wanders Boot Hill. The cemetery is home to numerous folks who met their ends in a violent manner—and they won't let anyone forget it, either. Among them are numerous victims of clubbings, lynchings, shootings, and knifings. In nearby Idaho City, an old grocery store hosts a shopper who peruses the shelves, then vanishes through the back wall. And Idaho City's oldest saloon, Diamond Lil's, has seen its share of thirsty spirits looking for spirits.

Marcus and Sophie Reynolds had agreed more than a year before that Idaho City and the surrounding region would be a great place to spend a honeymoon. Their friends thought they were nuts, but the young couple didn't have much money. However, Marcus did have an interest in the Old West and in old mining towns, in particular (he also had a gold pan he wanted to try out).

And Sophie had a serious urge to do some ghost hunting, albeit at a low-cost level. None of that fancy audio meter stuff for her, just a digital camera and a desire to see a spook. They each had good hiking boots and a backpack for carrying snacks, flashlights, and water. And on the first full day of their three-day visit to the region, they found themselves outside the Pioneer Cemetery, reading a sign that said, in part, ESTABLISHED DURING THE EARLY PART OF THE GOLD RUSH, AN ESTIMATED THREE THOUSAND PEOPLE LIE BURIED HERE. NOW, LESS THAN THREE HUNDRED OF THOSE HISTORIC GRAVES ARE IDENTIFIABLE.

"Oh," said Sophie. "That is so sad."

"Yeah," said Marcus. "But they chose to live here, right? I mean, you make your own luck in life."

"You're cranky because all we've been doing all day is looking at supposedly haunted sites and you haven't had a chance to try out your new gold pan."

Marcus shrugged.

"How about we go pan for some gold while we still have daylight, then later tonight, after a burger and a beer, we can go back to Boot Hill Cemetery. Lots of possibilities there."

"Now that sounds like the best plan you've had all day," he said. "Especially the burger-and-a-beer part. Count me in."

Later that night, after having told their waitress what they intended, she mentioned how some folks regretted visiting Boot Hill after dark.

"Why's that?" Marcus asked, more to be polite than out of interest. He'd finished his beer and wished he had another, in no hurry to sit in the dark and wait for something that probably wouldn't happen.

"Because of the ghosts," said the waitress.

Sophie leaned forward. "Really? What kind?"

"Misty-looking things, mostly. But lots of folks have caught sounds like whispering and footsteps on their recorders. And some folks see strange streaks of light, lots of orbs on photos." The waitress leaned in and spoke in a lowered voice, but she was smiling. "And on nights when there's no odd weather, you'll get mist, too. Others have seen ghosts of prospectors throughout the cemetery, looking like they're a little confused, lost maybe. And some visitors have heard odd lingo—come to find out it's Chinese they're hearing. There were tons of Chinese folks here, came to work the mines, in the laundries, restaurants, the works."

Marcus smiled as Sophie hopped to her feet. "You pay the bill," she said. "I have to go check my camera and the flashlights, make sure all the batteries are set."

He just nodded, amazed that this woman, his new wife, could not only believe in something as silly as ghosts, but get so excited about the possibility. Still, he was just as guilty, because he had a surprise for her.

He laughed as he met her in the parking lot. "Ready for some ghostbustin', sweetie?"

"Har har, make fun all you want, but we're going to Boot Hill tonight and we're going to see us a ghost or two. I can just tell."

"What do we do if we hear them but don't see them?"

"Well"—she bit her lip—"I don't have any way of recording them. But with two of us, we can at least corroborate each other's story."

Marcus smiled wide and pulled a wrapped present from out of his coat pocket. "I've been waiting to give you this, thought it might be an appropriate time."

"What's this? I don't have any more gifts for you."

"That's fine. I love the gold-panning gear you got me. This is just a little something I thought you might be able to use."

Like a little kid at Christmas Sophie tore open the wrap and found a hand-held high-sensitivity recorder inside. Perfect for capturing ghostly sounds.

"Oh, Marcus. Thank you so much—this is perfect. Just what we'll need tonight!" She hugged him and gave him a long, lingering smooch.

"Look now, you keep that up and we'll miss out on Boot Hill."

"Not on your life, mister," she said, checking out her new ghost-hunting gadget. "You drive and I'll figure out how to use this. It's this road, just northeast of town."

Two hours later found them leaning against the tree she'd chosen when they arrived. They were both wide awake and not a little nervous. Even Marcus, especially considering all the stories they'd read and heard about spooky sightings taking place where they were now sitting—in the middle of a dark night. And then Marcus felt Sophie's elbow jam into his arm.

He almost said, "Hey!" when he caught sight of the same thing she'd seen. It was the unmistakable apparition of a man, walking a few inches above the sparse grass, one hand scratching the side of his head as if in deep concentration. He was no more than twenty-five feet away and they watched him as he walked right at—and then through—several grave markers and one dilapidated picket enclosure. He made no sound, but they knew he was a ghost because they could see through him. It seemed as if he was made of light, though they could still make out details of his clothing.

Marcus nudged Sophie and nodded at her camera, sitting unused on its strap around her neck. She picked it up with shaking hands and tried to make it work; all the while the old ghostly prospector shuffled by them slowly. Finally Marcus heard the familiar click of the shutter button, once, twice, three times . . . and then he was gone.

Neither of them spoke, but they kept their eyes wide open and constantly swiveled their heads. They both wanted to check the camera to see if she'd gotten a picture of him, but they didn't dare—time enough for that later. In less than a half hour they heard a voice from far off but drawing nearer.

"Great," groaned Marcus in a whisper. "More ghost hunters. Or worse, kids partying."

"Shh," said Sophie. "I don't think so." She clicked on her new recorder and gave Marcus a quick stare to tell him not to talk. The voice drew nearer, and they traded looks again, eyes wide. It was someone speaking Chinese, but it sounded like an old radio fading in and out, in and out. This time Sophie had the gadget on and poised, its built-in microphone aimed at the general vicinity of the fading voice. Soon the voice faded out altogether.

They waited another half hour, but despite their amazing experiences they both began to yawn and decided to call it a night. By the time they got back to their hotel room, they were both wide awake again. They sat down together to check out the digital images and the audio recordings. The pictures weren't a total disappointment, but where the ghostly shuffling man had been now there was an orb of light and a streak tailing off of it.

"Could have been the camera," said Sophie, disappointed.

"No worries. I know what we saw," said Marcus. "And I know what we heard."

And with that they turned on the audio sounds she captured. And they were there, the unmistakable sound of someone speaking what sounded a lot like Chinese.

"Who's going to believe us?" asked Sophie.

"Anybody who wants to—and if they don't, well, that's their loss." Marcus smiled at Sophie.

When gold was first discovered in 1862 in the Boise Basin, no one had any idea of the amount that soon would be discovered. The figure is astounding: $100 million worth (and some sources claim upward of $250 million!), more than all the gold ever found in Alaska. And Lewiston became the capital of this region of unbelievable burgeoning wealth. But rapidly growing Bannock City, now known as Idaho City, soon became home to six thousand gold-hungry diggers.

In fewer than three years, the burg's population swelled to ten thousand and included all the amenities (and more) one might expect to spring up wherever hardworking, hard-playing miners congregated. More than 250 businesses vied for the weary miners' hard-earned dust, including an opera house, theaters, breweries, forty-one saloons, dance halls, gambling parlors, drug stores, brothels, a newspaper, and twenty-three law offices that dealt with claim disputes among hotheaded miners. And such arguments often resulted in violent action.

Idaho City's history is filled to brimming with accounts of armed men, cranked up on liquor and a drunk's sense of justice. Petty squabbles over card games or ill-fitting opinions often led to impromptu necktie parties, six-gun showdowns, fistfights, and back-alley guttings. It is believed that a good many victims—especially those killed for no real reason—continue to rove the places they were interred. Some eyewitnesses of the Boot Hill specters say they don't feel frightened or threatened by them, but they do feel as if there is a great sense of sadness in the air, a palpable melancholia exuded by the wispy visions as they drift among and through the old tombstones and fences surrounding some of the gravesites.

In addition to violence instigated by man, a series of brutal fires all but wiped out the town. Roughly 80 percent of the town had been razed, but unlike other burnt mining burgs, Idaho City was rebuilt each time because the gold hadn't yet played out. Diseases also took their toll on the town's bursting population. Many of those who eventually succumbed to their afflictions had been housed at the County Jail and Pest House, which dates from 1864 and is still standing.

No one knows what claimed the life of the young Chinese girl whose ghost has been seen many times standing beside a tombstone in the Chinese section of Pioneer Cemetery. Perhaps she is one of the last of three Chinese residents whose graves were not exhumed. The contents of those graves were sent to China, the most recent in 1993.

In places Boot Hill Cemetery is an overgrown tangle of undergrowth and tall pines—some have grown within various graves' enclosures, giving visitors an idea of how old the cemetery is—and is home to roughly two hundred dead, only two dozen of whom are claimed to have died of natural causes. Enclosures of many still-identifiable grave sites are little more than sagging ruins, picket fencing slowly being reclaimed by nature. Many of the carved wood markers and headstones tell how the resident happened to be there: a shooting, a lynching, or worse.

Not all the ghosts are maudlin, however. The oldest saloon in town, Diamond Lil's, which dates from 1862 and still serves a living clientele, also apparently does a brisk trade with those decidedly less alive. Numerous customers have witnessed the gauzy ghosts of old-time gamblers and miners quaffing a brew or two, no doubt relaxing after reliving their eternal days of hard labor digging for elusive ghostly gold.

Chapter 11

Oregon's
Forbidden Ground

The Oregon Vortex
Gold Hill, Oregon

Indians refer to the spot as the "Forbidden Ground." In 1864 whites settled there and felt extreme unease. Horses and other animals would not venture too near the site. Scottish physicist John Litster called it "aberrations in the light field and gravity." On the site, the House of Mystery, a former assay office, collapsed sideways in a violent thunderstorm. Photographs appear distorted, and visitors see the ghost of John Litster leaning in the doorway of the old cabin, laughing and plucking at his eyebrows before he disappears.

"There is a strange force here. We must go around." The tall, lean man motioned with his chin toward the seemingly normal treed, rocky hunk of land before them.

His companion, a rough cob of a mountain man named "Digger" Jones, was about to say something to humiliate Flaps-on-Wings, his Indian friend, but a feeling of raw uneasiness overcame him. He felt as if he were being watched, as if something like a pair of long, cold hands were creeping up his insides, from his bowels to his throat, leaving behind a trail of ice.

Despite this, Digger said, "This is foolish. I have places to go and things to do, and I am no Indian. Therefore, your ways and beliefs hold no sway over me." He sniffed and with his eyes fixed forward, so as to avoid the glaring gaze of Flaps-on-Wings—who frankly could be downright annoying at times and not a little preachy with all that Indian mumbo jumbo—urged his sorrel onward. They had advanced but a dozen feet when the horse balked. And the more Digger fought the neighing beast on the matter, the more it resisted.

Digger caught Flaps-on-Wings's knowing glance. "Don't say anything. Horse is spooked by something, is all. Likely a critter I didn't see scurried across our path."

But soon enough it became apparent that the horse wouldn't budge a step farther across the clearing. "Why, that's the trail, horse! That's where it leads!" He looked around in exasperation. "What in the world is wrong with this beast?"

But already Flaps-on-Wings was gently guiding his own horse fifty feet away from Digger, who, it seemed to Flaps-on-Wings, was doing his darnedest to guide his own horse *toward* the forces that were causing such grief. *Whites,* thought the Indian. *I will never understand their need to force nature to bend to their will.*

Finally Digger reined the ornery beast tight and under control. Then he sat on the horse, watched the Indian's back as he rode off, slightly southward from where the trail had been leading them, and said nothing. It was not in Digger's nature to ignore an opportunity to poke fun at his Indian companion, but somehow he felt the man was right. It galled him to admit it, but there was something odd about this place. "I don't know rightly what it means, but I guess I agree," mumbled Digger.

Flaps-on-Wings stopped from where he'd been cutting a wide circle around the place, but said nothing as he waited for his friend.

If Digger had been expecting some sort of conversation, he was once again mistaken. Finally Digger sighed and reined his own mount over beside the Indian. "You mind telling me why it is these ornery critters will walk over here"—he sluiced a stream of chaw juice at the mat of leaves and pine needles beside his horse—"but not over yonder? We ain't but fifty feet from there."

Flaps-on-Wings said nothing for a long minute, just staring at the place.

Digger sighed again, used to his friend's long, measured silences, convinced they were meant solely to annoy him. Finally he said, "Okay, Mister Wistful, I hope you're about ready to talk, 'cause I'm 'bout ready to listen."

Finally Flaps-on-Wings looked at him and said, "This is the Forbidden Ground. It has been so since before my people came here. The animals all know it." He turned to face Digger. "And so, my people came to know it."

Digger rasped a gnarled hand across his bearded face. "Well, sir, I'll give you this much. It sure do make me feel odd, sort of tetchy and uneasy like. Way down deep in my innards. I expect the horses feel the same. But what causes it?"

The Indian looked at his friend and raised his eyebrows, looking upward without moving his head.

"Okay, okay, the Great Spirit, eh? Well, by jiminy, if I ain't gonna get a straight answer out of your hide, I reckon I'll be moseying on, then. I had hoped to get a few miles under my belt by nightfall. And when I get to wherever it is I'm headed, I have a mind to get good and liquored up after this. Place makes me feel downright moody and broody, sort of like being stuck under a capsized canoe on a lake, only not so comfortable. If you know what I mean."

Flaps-on-Wings looked uptrail and said nothing as they rode north. With each step they took away from the place, Digger's mood lightened. "I don't rightly know what it was about the place that bothered my horse so, but never let it be said that Digger whupped on his horse unduly. As for me, well, I will admit there's just something wrong with that place, but by God if it don't rankle me to play a weak-kneed baby girl because a horse gets it into his head he's spooked by something that turns out to be its own shadow."

A horse-length ahead, Flaps-on-Wings smiled.

The chief assayer for the Old Grey Eagle Mining Company scratched his head as he surveyed the wreckage before him. And he wondered for the thousandth time whether the mine company hadn't made a mistake in setting up shop on this spot in 1904, six years before. After all, they'd been warned by Indians and local whites who all swore that the place was some sort of nexus of foul spirits or some such foofaraw.

Or at least that's what they'd thought of the warnings when they built the assayer's office here. The place had since been more trouble than it was worth. Half the time, miners were forever complaining because the scales seemed so inaccurate. Of course, the other half of the time, they said nothing because the scales tipped inexplicably in their favor.

But now look at it, he thought, walking around the place. As if all the weird things that had happened to him when he was here weren't bad enough: things disappearing, rocks looking like they rolled uphill, his workers looking short one minute, then walking a few paces and looking taller than they ever had. Made him want to wear spectacles. Except that other people saw the same weird things happen. *At least I know I'm not losing my mind,* he thought.

The little building hadn't been leaning the day before when he left for the day. But what had happened to it during that thunderstorm? What could possibly make a whole building slide off its foundation like that? Looked almost like it had half collapsed. But it was still upright, oddly enough. And stranger still, it seemed stable. He climbed inside and stared at the shambles of everything—his desk had slid the length of the cabin and slammed into the far wall, glass jars were broken and sacks of ore samples overturned, his scales and tools all jumbled, and the entire workbench had become dislodged and lay at angles across the room. The windows had puckered and burst, but the structure itself still seemed stout, not a weak spot in the floor, almost as if someone had built it on purpose to tease and taunt the human mind. The assayer lifted his cap and scratched his head again. It sure was a mystery.

Dulcie, the tour guide, waited until everyone in her group had gathered around her in the little cabin before she continued her well-rehearsed spiel. "Welcome to the inside of Oregon's House of Mystery, which sits on the site of the Oregon Vortex. Those of you who may be more sensitive than others will already know what I am about to tell you: This place is one of the few spots in the world with an abnormally high level of energy. For countless centuries, local Indian tribes called it the 'Forbidden Ground' and would take great pains to avoid riding too close here due to the high level of unease it can create in a person. Don't be embarrassed if you, too, feel it."

She paused and watched the group for signs of early alarm. Once in a while she'd get someone who would look ready to scream. She always tried to get the person to a quiet spot away from the vortex before their fear spread throughout the group.

"Early white settlers to the region trekking out here for the gold—this place is called Gold Hill, after all—also reported feeling uneasy when near here, and there are several journal entries of travelers at the time who referred to the place as having, in their words, 'something wrong' with it." The tour guide smiled at the group, then continued. "The building dates from 1904, when the Old Grey Eagle Mining Company built it on this site as an assay office. One night, after a particularly violent electrical thunderstorm, the building was knocked off its foundation and came to rest as you see it today, seemingly as stout as the day it was built—just crooked.

"In 1914 a Scottish physicist named John Litster visited the site and never really left—literally. He's still here. Or rather his ghost is. We'll get to that in a minute. But when he was alive, he studied what he called 'aberrations in the light field and gravity.' The vortex is a strong whirling energy mass that resides on this site that is 165 feet in diameter." Dulcie made a broad sweep with her hands. "Half above ground and half in ground, with the center of it just behind the building, right out there. Often pictures taken within the vortex, and especially behind the building, where it's strongest, will appear distorted and wavy. People standing inside the vortex tend to lean at an unnatural angle of approximately 7.5 degrees, even though they think that they're standing upright. Litster himself was so baffled by this place that he stayed and studied it until his death in 1959.

"The Indians considered this site sacred and took great pains to leave it alone. There have been numerous reports over the years of people witnessing and experiencing paranormal activity. You'll note there are not a lot of animals here."

She paused, and watched as the people in the group looked around, as if expecting to see a mouse or a cougar and prove her wrong. "That's because they refuse to go near the vortex—and rightly so. They seem to know something the rest of us don't."

Though John Litster's corporeal body may have left the place, his ghost has been seen numerous times, mostly inside the House of Mystery, where he has often been seen leaning in the door frame, a knowing smile on his face. He has even appeared in family vacation photos taken there. Many people have all seen the same thing: an old man, smiling, wearing out-of-date clothes, sometimes laughing and plucking at his eyebrows. Then he fades from view.

Energy, spiritual or otherwise, is at the center of the still unsolved mystery of the Oregon Vortex. The odd location has been said to possess anomalies in gravity, convolutions in the earth's magnetic field, and a wellspring or concentration of paranormal energy. Visitors often feel intense vertigo, and animals won't venture inside the place. And Native Americans still refer to it as the "Forbidden Ground." Despite these facts, the site opened as a tourist attraction in 1930 and has continued as such since then, with thousands of people visiting each year, unsure when they get there of just what they'll feel . . . or who they'll see.

Part Three

HOTEL, BROTHEL & SALOON

Chapter 12

Hauntings at
the Hot Springs

Chico Hot Springs Resort & Day Spa
Pray, Montana

Pray, Montana's famous Chico Hot Springs offers visitors world-class dining, comfy accommodations, luxurious hot springs in which to soak—and a specter in a white dress, one Percie Knowles, wife of Chico's builder. She's been seen, followed, and photographed, and appears to be part of the place—at least in spirit. There's also an antique rocking chair that always faces a window, no matter where it's placed. And a family Bible, opened on a wooden bench in the attic, never gathers dust.

"Some folks call her the 'Lady in White,'" said the house-maid to the newly hired summer girl. "I ain't seen her, but I know a couple of security guards who have. 'Course, I have had some experiences, particularly on the third floor, that you might call odd. Up there alone one day I was, and I heard footsteps, like shoes on a wood floor, then a door slammed. I swallowed hard, I'll tell you. And it took all my strength to leave the room I was cleaning and investigate."

The new girl said nothing, but her eyes grew wide and she stopped folding the white guest towels. "What happened?"

"Don't stop working as I talk to you, or your summer of employment here will be mighty short, girl."

The red-faced girl resumed folding, eager to hear the story, but more eager to make a sound impression on her first day at Chico Hot Springs Lodge and Ranch. She'd heard about the famous resort, certainly, being a local girl from Bozeman, an hour west of Chico's pretty location in Paradise Valley outside the town of Pray.

After a couple minutes of silent work, cleaning one of the guest cabins, the older woman said, "Oh, turns out it was Room 49, Percie's old room. I knew it would be."

"Who's Percie?"

"I'm getting to that. And make sure you don't work those towels so much they lose their fluff. Guests pay good money to stay here; they like to be pampered."

"Yes, ma'am." The girl kept working, occasionally glancing up at the other woman.

Finally the older woman spoke. "A few years back, them two security guards even took a picture of her." She looked at the girl. "The ghost, I mean."

"Really? What does she look like?"

"Well, in the picture, not so much. Just sort of a white dot of light. But what they saw was mostly the top half of a young lady wearing a white dress. She was in the lounge, by the piano."

"Do they know who she is . . . or was?"

"Like I said, near as anyone can tell, it's Percie Knowles. She and her husband built the place back in the 1890s. Did all right for a while, I guess, but he ended up drinking himself to death. She did what she could, held on for a while. They had a boy, but he ended up leaving. So she ran the place as a hospital and sanitarium, but eventually she lost money. Can't get along without the money that booze brings in, I guess. Anyways, you get yourself an encounter with her, then you'll be a member of what we call 'the Percie Club.'"

Among employees of Chico, there have been many members of the Percie Club over the years. Security guards in particular have had extensive interactions with her ghost, and that of her husband, too. One such guard, alone at Chico on an overnight shift in January 1990, knew there were no guests on the third floor that week. While making his rounds in the wee hours, he passed by the stairwell that led to the third floor and he sensed a presence at the top of the stairs. He looked up—there stood a woman in a dress staring down at him. He assumed she was a guest unable to sleep. He asked if he could help her, but she turned and glided away.

The guard followed, but the third-floor hallway was dark and no one was in sight. Since he knew all the rooms on that floor to be locked, he walked down the hall and smelled a fragrance that reminded him of jasmine or lilac, especially strong near Rooms 346 through 350, and strongest before Room 349. He keyed into the room and as his flashlight shone over the room's interior, he noted that the rocking chair near the window was swinging gently. He switched on the room's light—the rocking stopped and the fragrance faded.

It stands to reason that the chair in that room would be in use, as Room 349 is where Percie Knowles spent much of her time during her last years alive at Chico, rocking and staring out the window, quietly slipping into senility.

Other security guards have had similar experiences. One fellow saw a misty figure slowly ascend the staircase to the third floor. She was clothed in a long white dress similar to the one Percie Knowles can be seen wearing in a photograph hanging in the lobby. The same guard also had the repeated and unnerving experience of finding Room 349 unlocked and the door open, no matter how many times he closed and locked it while on his rounds. This proved especially vexing to him, as he was the only one on the premises with the keys, and no guests were on that floor at the time.

This guard also witnessed a man and a woman sitting at a table in the lounge after hours one night. He assumed it was one of the staff or family of the owner, but when he glanced back and made to enter the lounge, the figures were gone. The woman had been wearing a long white dress. It was assumed by most folks familiar with the ghostly goings-on at Chico that the couple was Bill and Percie Knowles.

Yet another night guard was surprised on a cold winter overnight shift at three a.m. . . .

Hank didn't mind being the only person at the hotel. Sometimes that happened in winter when bookings were slow. Even when the power had gone out for a couple of hours the week before, he'd been calm, taking care of what needed attending to. Heck, even knowing that there were ghosts about the place didn't bother him. And tonight was no different, he decided, though it was bitterly cold. He poked at the settling logs in the fireplace once again and added another before extending his chapped hands toward the flames. And that's when the crashing and clanging of pots and pans from the kitchen pulled him upright.

He snatched up his heavy flashlight and headed toward the noise. As he approached the kitchen, the sounds stopped with the speed of a finger snap. He narrowed his eyes, held his breath, and burst through the door, fully expecting to catch a couple of thieves in the act of rummaging through the kitchen—for what purpose, he wasn't sure.

But when he flicked on the lights, a blast of cold air washed over him. Across the room he saw a woman in a long dress with her back to him. But this was no ordinary woman—she floated six inches above the floor. He'd seen some interesting women in his day, but none who could pull off such a feat. He watched her for a few minutes, then she moved off, opened a nearby door that had been padlocked from the outside, and was gone. Hank waited a few moments, noticing that the temperature in the room had begun to warm up again. He checked the door from the inside, aware that he was the only person on the premises with a key. It was locked tight and appeared to not have been opened for some time. A careful check of the outdoors revealed no footsteps and no indication that the door had been opened. Hank went back inside and warmed his hands by the fire, fully aware now that he'd become a member of the Percie Club.

Bill and Percie Knowles married in 1891 and within a few short years saw the benefits of establishing a boardinghouse near the naturally occurring warm springs, as they were referred to in those days. They rented rooms to miners for six dollars a week. Business was brisk for the Knowles, and by 1900 they opened a hotel on the spot.

Soon, over the protests of his wife, Bill Knowles built an adjoining dance hall and saloon, and the place became even more popular. But close proximity to all that fun and booze appeared to be too great a temptation to Bill Knowles.

He came down with a fatal case of cirrhosis of the liver and died in 1910. Percie was left with their twelve-year-old son, Radbourne, and the business.

She promptly shut down the saloon she so despised and reopened the establishment as a health center. And for a decade or so, it seemed like a good decision. She hired a doctor and eventually transformed the place yet again into a sanitarium. Her son left to pursue his own life and Percie, managing the place and a staff of nurses all alone, sagged then cracked under the burden of a failing business. Her staff thought highly of her, however, and took care of her as she convalesced in Room 49 (now 349) on the third floor. But she did not recuperate. Instead she slowly lost her sanity and was moved to a mental hospital, where she died several years later, in 1940.

Since then, and despite the fact that Chico has had a series of owners, it has become apparent to employees—and to a number of guests as well—that Percie Knowles returned to her beloved hot springs resort shortly after her death. She seems to spend much of her time on the third floor, particularly in her old room, but she does visit the attic and other locations throughout the lodge.

No matter where it is moved, a rocking chair in her room always ends up facing the window through which can be seen Emigrant Peak, a favored view of Mrs. Knowles. She is also said to tend to a Bible on a bench in the attic. Always open to the same page in Psalms, the pages remain dust free. Employees have flipped to other passages, but when they return, the book is open to Percie's preferred page in Psalms.

Other spiritual activity has been felt about the place, most notably in the kitchen and dining room, where plates and silverware move without cause. And in the employees' rooms, staff members have several times awakened to feel the presence of someone sitting on their bed, watching them while they sleep. Could the Knowleses just be continuing their living roles as caretakers more than a century after their beloved resort's heyday?

Despite, or perhaps in part because of, Chico Hot Springs' paranormal peculiarities, the resort is larger and more popular than ever. And the primary draw, the hot springs themselves, are still very much in use. Year-round, guests enjoy a long, hot soak before indulging in one of Chico's world-famous gourmet dining experiences (and perusing its extensive, award-winning wine list). The hotel also offers spa facilities, cabins for families, a larger separate hotel annex, horseback riding, and much more. It's not uncommon to rub elbows in the hot springs or in the dining room with Hollywood stars. And who knows? You might even meet the original owners of the place.

Chapter 13
The Swamper

Big Nose Kate's Saloon
Tombstone, Arizona

Known as the Grand Hotel until the 1980s, the business was owned by Big Nose Kate, aka Mary Katherine Harmony, in Tombstone's mining heyday of the 1880s. Once the home of her paramour, famed gambling gunman Doc Holliday, the hotel brims with the ghosts of cowboys content sitting at the bar, leaning in doorways, and playing petty pranks. And then there's the Swamper, the ghost of an employee who dug a tunnel in the basement that connected to a mine's vein of rich silver. Rumor has it that he still protects his stash.

"Oh, don't pay him no mind." The stout woman winked at the cowboy and slid the filled beer mug over to him. "That's just the Swamper. He's, well, he's our swamper."

"That his name?" asked the cowboy, sipping the foam from the beer.

"Well, no, but that's what we call him. Swamper."

"Swamper's usually a man who cleans up the place, empties spittoons, mops the floor, that sort of thing."

"And that's what he does here. He's a handyman, fixes up things. Don't ask for much, just a place to hole up. He's set himself up in the basement." She wiped the bar top.

"You let him stay down there?"

"Sure. He says he likes it down there. Says it reminds him of all the time he spent underground working the mines."

Just out of hearing range, the man known to Tombstone as the Swamper paused in the doorway to the basement, his eyes squinting as he listened, chewing the ragged edges of his moustache. Satisfied that no one was following him, he descended the stairs to the basement and his demure quarters in the corner. He paused a moment, listening to hear whether anyone had followed, then eased his hands behind the wooden bedframe and lifted it a few feet to the side.

In the back corner behind his bed, he used a long, bent nail and pried at the bottom corner of a wooden panel, a panel that looked like nothing more than part of the stone and wood walls lining the basement. He hefted the panel free and set it within easy reach. Should someone come down, he wanted to be able to replace it quickly.

Next he flared a match and lit an oil lantern, adjusted the wick height, and held the wire bail aloft in front of him. The Swamper smiled as the light reached into the cold, still blackness of the small tunnel he'd dug in the wall. It had taken him many months, but now it was paying off. He had managed to connect to a feeder tunnel that led to the Toughnut Mine. And no one knew he was working it when everyone else was asleep.

Just about all of Tombstone had tunnels running under it. And he knew for a fact quite a few of the buildings with basements, many of them little more than root cellars, had been dug farther to provide access to mine shafts and tunnels. Why should the Grand Hotel be any different? Just because he was the swamper and all-around handyman didn't mean he couldn't take advantage of his basement dwelling to do a little digging in his spare time.

He liked the job just fine and figured that Ms. Harmony was satisfied with his work, since she wasn't complaining to him. All the more reason for them to leave him alone. He'd built up his own little hidey-hole in the corner of the basement and most folks didn't bother with him.

All his hard work had been paying off. He'd been storing up nuggets of high-grade silver ore for months. Only problem he had was getting it to an assayer who didn't know him. Seems like even in a bustling place like Tombstone someone knew someone who knew you. And in the end, they'd probably trace his finds to his basement digs. But he couldn't have that. Not yet anyway. In the meantime, he'd keep on working for Ms. Harmony (the sporting men called her Big Nose Kate), and hope like heck that no one got wind of his work.

He'd tried to keep the noise to a minimum, but sometimes in the middle of the night when it seemed the world was asleep, and the saloons had quieted, he swore the steady *clunk clink clank* of his pick and the scrape of his shovel could be heard all over town. He knew he was imagining this, of course, but for the time being he would continue to stash his ore in sacks. He'd already buried two and secreted a third in another part of the wall.

No sir, he had a good thing going on here as fixer-upper of the Grand—might as well stick with it until he had enough to really do it up in style, to leave on good terms and with a fortune in silver earnings in the bank. He just knew he'd soon be rich. "Rich, I tell you," he said aloud, and let out a soft chuckle.

But the Swamper's smile was short-lived, for his thoughts turned, as they always did, to his carefully stashed ore. He would do whatever it took to protect it. For as long as it took.

"It's a slow-as-mud night in the middle of the off-season," said the owner of Big Nose Kate's. "What say we poke around the Swamper's diggins? I've never even been down into 'em."

"What do you think we'll see?" The bartender was already moving out from behind the bar, up for an adventure—especially on such a boring evening.

"I, for one, would like to know if it really does connect with the Toughnut Mine shaft. And I wouldn't cry if I found a rich vein of silver while I was at it."

"Then count me in," said the barmaid.

Outfitted with flashlights and a few nervous laughs, the trio headed down to the basement, to the Swamper's old living quarters. They made their way into the tunnel and slowly explored its dark, dry depths. It didn't take them long to confirm what they'd always been told: The shaft did indeed connect with the Toughnut. Other than that, there wasn't much more for them to see.

As they made their way back to the basement, they heard a loud moan, as if someone had just discovered they'd lost something valuable, then hurried footsteps slammed down the basement stairs, toward them. The three explorers stopped in their tracks.

"Someone's in the basement," whispered the bartender.

"Can't be," said the owner. "I locked the doors."

Skeptical, the bartender pushed by them and ran into the basement but saw no one. He bolted up the basement stairs but again saw no one. They all went upstairs and checked the doors and all the rooms, but found no one anywhere inside the place, and the doors were still locked.

"Well," said the owner, smiling at his companions. "Looks like we upset the Swamper." But it would be awhile before they laughed about the experience.

A tourist from New Jersey guided her son into the front door of Big Nose Kate's and slipped her white-frame sunglasses off, tucked them on top of her head, and let her eyes adjust to the dark interior of the place. It wasn't yet busy, but it had come recommended as a great spot for a burger.

Her son, Tommy, decked out in a spiffy blue cowboy hat and wearing orange-tipped six-guns in a plastic gun belt, gazed across the room. She leaned over and followed her son's pointing hand toward the bar across the room. "Look, Ma. It's a real cowboy. See, standing at the bar? Just like in a real Old West saloon on TV."

A passing waitress, hands filled with menus and a tray of drinking glasses, said, "That's 'cause this is a real, honest-to-God Old West saloon, son." She winked at the boy.

His mother reddened and started to apologize, but the waitress kept on walking.

"Well, anyway, Tommy, he's probably here for people like us."

"Can I talk to him, Ma?"

His mother squinted into the dark. "Well, I suppose it couldn't hurt. I could take your picture with him while we wait for your father, then we'll have lunch and—"

"And then we go on the OK Corral tour! The man at the store said they really shoot during it, too."

"I know, honey."

The little boy walked toward the cowboy standing at the far end of the bar. But then Tommy slowed, hesitated, then stopped altogether.

"What's wrong, Tommy?"

But the boy didn't reply. He stopped and stared at the cowboy. Then his mother stood staring at the cowboy, too, as the tall, see-through wrangler turned toward them, touched his hat brim, and vanished.

The Grand Hotel was once one of the most sumptuous hotels in the Southwest, with sixteen rooms, all with windows, thick imported carpets, original oil paintings on the walls, and lavishly upholstered walnut furniture, chandeliers, a modern kitchen with running hot and cold water, and a popular bar on the ground floor. It officially opened on September 9, 1880. Unfortunately, it was a short-lived grandeur, as the hotel nearly burned to the ground on May 25, 1882—the date of a sizable conflagration that razed a number of buildings in Tombstone.

However, during its brief run the Grand Hotel housed not only Doc Holliday and his companion, the hotel's owner, prostitute Big Nose Kate, aka Mary Katherine Harmony, but Wyatt and Virgil Earp also stayed there, as did the Clantons and McLaurys. Indeed the latter two parties spent the evening before the infamous "shootout at the OK Corral" at the Grand.

After the fire, it was rebuilt and roughly resembled the shorter structure it is today. The original long bar was rescued and is still in use at Big Nose Kate's. And one can still order beers, dine, and shop at the establishment named for the woman who many believe was, along with her sister, the first prostitute to set up shop in the new boom town known as Tombstone in 1880.

The Swamper's rough accommodation in the basement, as well as his secretly dug tunnel that connected to the

Toughnut Mine, still exist and are a popular visitor attraction. But visitors are forewarned that lots of folks have felt the eerie presence or seen the ghost of the wizened old Swamper. Several employees have felt cold, wet hands encircling their throats while in the basement. There have also been reported sightings of cowboys leaning on the bar or standing in doorways, as if they had just ridden into town for a beer and to loaf away the afternoon hours watching foot traffic.

The ghost of one cowboy, apparently irate, is said to have knocked over cases of beer in the basement. Maybe he was looking for the Swamper's silver. Glasses have been seen to move of their own accord on the polished bar top, silverware spins and flies off tables, doors open and close with no assistance from (living) hands, and light fixtures flicker on and off with no switches having been used.

It is said the Swamper's ghost roams the basement unceasingly, fretting over his stashed silver, and that he is very protective of it. Cowboys and the hazy image of an old miner have appeared in photographs taken by tourists, who are both terrified and thrilled—and torn as to whether they might return to the chillingly haunted saloon known as Big Nose Kate's in downtown Tombstone.

Other haunted spots in this infamous Old West town include the Bird Cage Theatre, called by the *New York Times* in 1882 "the wildest, wickedest night spot between Basin Street and the Barbary Coast." This burlesque hall was open for only nine years, but oh, what a nine years: Sixteen raging gunfights left 140 bullet holes pocking the walls and ceiling while prostitutes worked the boxes. Today the voices of dozens of spirits and spooks have been heard by tourists and locals.

Nellie Cashman's Restaurant (Nellie was a renowned friend of miners and all-around do-gooder) is home to a number of nuisance-making cowboys and miners. They have been witnessed moving and breaking various objects as if they enjoy the loud, crashing sounds.

The ghosts of Schieffelin Hall (named after the founder of Tombstone and finder, in 1877, of the first big silver strike, Ed Schieffelin) appear to become riled when the hall is used for various civic meetings. The Wells Fargo Building is known to be haunted by apparitions of stagecoach drivers and cowboys. And in the street out front, a tall man wearing a broad black hat and traditional Old West frock coat has been seen numerous times crossing the street. But he never reaches the other side, vanishing before he steps up onto the sidewalk.

And one of the Old West's most famous cemeteries, Tombstone's Boot Hill, is filled with graves of famous and infamous folk, including Clantons and McLaurys, and a number of victims of shootings, stabbings, disease, and hangings. Many of them seem to like it so well that even in the afterlife they roam the place, popping up now and again in photos, looking quite concerned, and not a little protective of their final resting place.

Chapter 14

Ghost Host of
the Bullock

The Historic Bullock Hotel
Deadwood, South Dakota

The spirit of famed lawman Seth Bullock haunts the Deadwood hotel he and his partner opened in 1896. Guests and staff have seen dishes and cutlery fly off tables, lights turn on and off by themselves, doors and shower curtains have minds of their own, broken clocks chime, cloudy images appear in photographs, and boots clunk and spurs jingle across wood floors. And many women have felt the light touch of amorous hands on their hips, and feel as if they're being watched when they brush their hair and shower. Not long ago a lost child was helped back to his room one night. The next day the boy identified the long-dead Bullock in a photo as the nice cowboy who had helped him.

"We won't be gone long. And look at him, he's sleeping like . . ."

"A baby," said his wife, without taking her eyes from her snoozing little boy.

"Honey," said her husband, "it's our last night here. I think we should hit the tables for a little gambling fun. We won't be gone long. Look, this place is safe as houses. And having the slots and tables just downstairs couldn't make it any easier for us, right?"

"Okay, but just for a little while."

The couple finished getting ready, she kissed her little boy on the forehead, and they went down to the casino to try their luck. A little while later, the boy awoke to the dim glow of a nightlight, and the odd feeling that he was alone in the hotel room. "Mommy? Daddy?"

No answer came to him, not like he was used to hearing. He began to whimper, and within minutes his whimpering turned into sobs. He checked the entire room, then the bathroom, and couldn't find his parents. And that's when he knew he was alone.

He opened the hotel room door and passed down the hallway, sobbing and rubbing tiny knuckles into his crying eyes. He made his way down one floor, crying louder for his parents. He wandered down yet another hallway, sobbing as he ran, desperate to find his mommy and daddy.

He turned a corner and bumped into a thin older man wearing cowboy boots, a black suit, and a cowboy hat, and across his face bristled a massive moustache. "Here, now. Here, here," the old man said, hunkering down and holding the boy by the shoulders. "What's all this commotion anyway? My stars, child, you're yelpin' loud enough to wake the dead." He smiled and gave the boy's arm a reassuring squeeze.

"I can't find my mommy and daddy."

"Well, that's okay, partner, because they're downstairs having a little fun with the cards. They'll be along shortly. I expect you're getting tired anyway, huh?"

The little boy felt himself grow sleepy; all that wandering and crying had taken its toll on him. He yawned and dragged a dimpled hand across his tear-streaked face.

The cowboy stood and placed a reassuring hand on the little boy's shoulder. "What say you and me find your room, get you put back in bed."

"Okay." The little boy headed back toward where he remembered their room was, the old cowboy at his side. There was something very comforting about the man. Every time the boy looked up, the tall cowboy was smiling down at him; his eyes were so very kind. He sort of reminded the boy of his grandfather.

Soon enough they came to the room and the little boy got settled into bed. "Thank you, mister."

The cowboy stood in the doorway, smiled, and said, "Why, you're welcome, partner. Sleep fast—mornin' comes quick." He winked and was gone.

The next morning, as they were checking out, the boy told his parents about what had happened. They weren't pleased that he'd been wandering the hotel looking for them. And they felt guilty, especially his father, who didn't dare meet his wife's reproachful gaze.

"But a really nice cowboy helped me," said the boy. "He told me you were okay and then he got me back to our room. I was so tired."

"Who was it, honey? Do you remember?" His mother tried not to show her mounting panic that a complete stranger had been with her boy—and put him to bed, too.

Before she could let that line of thought play out, the little boy smiled and said, "That's him, that's the man who helped me." He was pointing toward the photograph of Seth Bullock that hangs on the wall in the hotel lobby.

The woman who worked the front desk didn't seem all that surprised. "Oh, good. That's Mr. Bullock. He built this place."

"But . . . ," said the father. "But this place was built a century ago."

The woman nodded as she slid the room receipt over the counter to him. "That's right," she said. "Your boy there had an encounter with Seth Bullock's ghost. He died in 1919. He's buried up on Mount Moriah, overlooking the town, but this is where he chooses to hang his hat, so to speak. I can't blame him; the Bullock was his pride and joy. Or still *is*, I should say."

She leaned toward the wide-eyed parents and in a lowered voice said, "I'm glad he's taken to helping youngsters. He's a bit of a ladies' man, you see. Often our female guests will awaken in the night to feel a hand resting on their . . . well, on their backsides. Never any tricky business, just a sort of reassuring love pat from a rakish old ghost. I can almost hear him laughing now, can't you?"

The parents exchanged wide-eyed glances. They didn't know quite what to think.

The new server came into the kitchen, her hand to her chest, her face white. She stood off to the side until the cook came over to the coffeepot. "What's wrong?"

"I . . . I think I've seen a ghost."

The cook smiled. "'Course you did. We told you that Seth Bullock is still here. A tall, thin cowboy?"

The new girl nodded, and the cook began to tell her about her own ghostly experiences, starting years back. She recalled her first week on the job at the Bullock Hotel. She'd taken a small break before her scheduled break time. She'd been alone in the kitchen at the time, so she figured she would have a quick pick-me-up cup of coffee. Something she couldn't see had nudged her, and at the same time, a teaspoon on the counter spun on its own, then flipped to the floor. That got her attention. She'd since been told that Mr. Bullock didn't like it when people shirked their duties, sang, or whistled while they worked. And he wasn't afraid to let the employees know it.

Just last year she'd heard ringing footsteps behind her in the hallway outside the kitchen, and for a second wasn't sure what that could mean. She turned, saw no one, and resumed walking. The peculiar ringing started again, and that's when she recognized it: boots with spurs. She'd seen enough cowboy movies to know that singular sound. She'd spun and saw nothing but an empty hallway. The footsteps ceased, then a man's low chuckle echoed down the hall, as if heard from the end of a long, hollow tube. Then that, too, faded.

She knew she should be used to such things. After all, she'd seen bottles and glasses slide along the bar, silverware leap off tables, and old antique clocks that hadn't worked in a century suddenly begin chiming out the hour. But for some reason those spurs and boot steps unnerved her. If none of the other things had happened, she'd not have told a soul. But she knew enough employees of the Bullock had had odd experiences that they wouldn't think her a crackpot.

"So you see, your experience isn't anything to worry over. Why, there are so many more I could tell you about."

The new girl's eyes widened. "Aren't the ones you've mentioned enough?"

"Sure, but those are just some of the things I've experienced since I started working here more years ago than I care to remember." She looked up from making a fresh pot of coffee. "You heard about that lady last month who woke up in the middle of the night with what felt like a man's hand on her hip?"

The new girl wrinkled her nose. "Husband?"

"Nope, not married. And she was alone in her room." The older woman's eyebrows rose and she smirked. "And then it patted her and she heard a man's chuckle."

The new girl swallowed. "And then?"

"What do you think happened? He left her in peace. Mr. Bullock is a gentleman, after all. Even if he is a ghost."

In 1876 Seth Bullock and his business partner, Sol Star, arrived in the lawless tent town of Deadwood, driving clanking and jostling wagons, each loaded to brimming with stoves, pans, pots, tools, and more, goods brought from their former hardware store in Helena, Montana. They set up shop on a prime corner lot on Main and Wall Streets and found rapid success.

The fire of 1879 damaged the store but didn't put them out of business. They soon built a new store with a brick warehouse behind. Things rolled along well until 1894, when another fire destroyed the store but left the warehouse intact. Instead of reinvesting in the hardware business, the partners erected a top-shelf hotel built of sandstone in Italianate style. When it opened its doors in April 1896, the Bullock Hotel offered a one hundred–seat restaurant that served lobster and fine game birds, a sumptuous lobby bedecked with carpeting, brass fixtures, and a grand piano, and a library for use by patrons. The sixty-three rooms upstairs offered brass beds, a bathroom on each floor, central heat, and hot and cold water. A few years later an adjoining building was purchased and made into the Gentlemen's Bar. During Bullock and Star's years of ownership, the hotel gained wide fame as one of the finest in the West.

The partners sold the business in 1904 and it continued throughout the twentieth century under a series of owners, becoming more timeworn as the years rolled by. In the 1990s it was purchased again and completely refurbished to its former grandeur, albeit with modern conveniences. Today the Bullock Hotel is the most photographed building in Deadwood, and not just because it has been handsomely restored.

In addition to becoming one of Deadwood's most successful businessmen, it soon came out that Seth Bullock, with his steely gaze and no-nonsense approach to lawbreakers, had worn a star in several other towns. He had a reputation as a fair man not given to whimsy or indulgence where hard work or criminals were involved. He became Deadwood's first sheriff, bringing rigid and much-needed backbone to a town previously thought untamable.

Not satisfied with all these accomplishments, Bullock started a successful ranch in nearby Belle Fourche—a town that he helped establish—and he also became Teddy Roosevelt's close friend. At the time of his death of colon cancer on September 23, 1919, at age seventy, Bullock was one of the most revered and famous men in all the West. He was buried at Mount Moriah Cemetery, on a bluff overlooking Mount Roosevelt, a mountain he had renamed to honor his dear friend Teddy Roosevelt after the Rough Rider's passing.

Even in death Seth Bullock is restless, and continues his lifelong habit of hard work and round-the-clock attentiveness, and this continues to make him one of the most famous characters in all the West, albeit a ghostly one. And if the numerous accounts by employees, patrons, and guests are any indication, he shows no signs of retiring anytime soon.

Chapter 15

The Longest
Night . . . Ever

The Phantom Saloon
Park County, Wyoming

In the mid-1800s, two line riders lost in a blinding blizzard stumbled on an old, dusty saloon. Confused by this building they knew shouldn't be there, they built a fire. Soon they saw a bartender staring at them, but he disappeared. Then the room filled with sound—laughter, glasses, poker chips, bottles clinking, piano music—but no one was there. Next morning, they rode for the ranch. No one believed them and the saloon was never seen again. Or if it was, other cowboys who found it in their hour of need haven't mentioned it. . . .

"My God, Rigby, we don't get in outta this weather, we're going to end up like them beeves—stuck fast in a drift, feet up, and heads froze solid. And we won't wake up again, neither." Horton looked over at the younger cowboy he'd been traveling the ranch's range with. If the young man heard him, he gave no indication.

They'd been riding the line for close to two months in increasingly hard weather. Seemed like it never let up. And now here they were, lost somewhere between line camps, a hard, stiff wind freezing everything it touched. He didn't know how his sorrel could stand it. The horses were beginning to show the effects of the weather, moving slower, heads bent low, but any lower and they'd not be able to keep from wallowing in the snow.

The men dismounted frequently and finally just accepted that they'd have to trudge on through, pulling the reins and urging their mounts forward with tugs and shouts. The wind sliced right through the scarves they'd swaddled around their hats, snugging the brims down over their ears. Their moustaches were caked with frozen icicles that hung over their mouths and grew with each breath they rasped out.

Yep, thought Horton, *this might be the one night we don't make it to a line camp. I do believe we've lost our way, and in this weather, that's a death sentence.* Then he caught sight of the younger cowboy eyeing him through slitted, snow-crusted eyes. Horton smiled at the youth. Or at least he tried to. "Might be we wanna turn back now, Rigby. This is fixing to blow us off the map!"

The young man nodded and they both looked back, into the wind, at where they'd just come from. And they wished they hadn't.

Any indication of where they'd been was long gone. Even the closest tracks just behind them were filling in almost as fast as they and their horses punched them through thigh-deep drifts. There was nothing there but white squalling blasts of snow falling fast from the sky. It blew in every direction at once, and it suddenly seemed colder than it had been in the previous two months.

"Ah! Horton! Look!"

The older cowboy pushed himself up off the horse's neck. It took most of his strength. There, before them and their horses' blowing, shuddering heads, was a building. The wind was gusting too hard to see it well, but Horton figured it was the line camp. *Of all the dumb, blind luck,* he thought.

We were as lost as lost can be, but we somehow stumbled on the one tiny outpost in hundreds of miles out here on the wind-stripped plain. By God . . .

If they had known what awaited them, Horton and Rigby might not have dismounted, might have chosen to stagger on into the teeth of the blizzard, even at the risk of dying in a snowdrift. But they had no way of knowing what sort of a night they were in for. . . .

The two men groped their way along the puckered, wind-dried wood of the sagging old structure, leading their horses as their numb hands explored the weathered boards inches from their faces. Halfway around they came to a lean-to that cut much of the wind, and with some effort and kicking through a stiffened snowdrift, they led their horses into the meager shelter.

As they continued around the side of the low structure, they searched for a door, all the while fighting blinding, driving snow and wind that blasted sudden gusts in their eyes. Their puzzlement at finding this previously unseen building—even a ramshackle structure—where before none had existed, was overshadowed by the prospect of finding any sort of shelter at all. For where there was such, there was the chance of survival, something that mere frozen minutes before had seemed impossible.

"I found it—a door!" yelled Rigby through chattering teeth. "Here, help me dig it out."

With clumsy, pawing efforts they pushed and knocked away enough snow that they could yank open the door. They wedged themselves through the scant opening. Once inside, they squinted into the cold, windowless space. Their breaths clouded the air, but soon their eyes grew more accustomed to the dark and they could make out vague shapes. On a low table against a wall to the right of the door, Horton's rag-wrapped, fumbling hands found an oil lamp and almost knocked the glass chimney from it. "Got any matches?"

The younger man did but could barely retrieve them from his pocket, so numbed by cold were his fingers. They finally managed, between the two of them and several broken stick matches later, to produce a meager flame. The dry, frayed end of wick caught fire and sparks skittered until the hungry flame reached the oil that had leached upward on the old wick. A warm glow lit the small space around them. And for long minutes the two chatter-teethed cowboys could do nothing more than stand huddled over the flame, their aching, cupped hands held just above its life-giving warmth.

"We got to kindle a real fire in that fireplace yonder, or we're done for, Rigby."

The two men reluctantly turned from the meager heat of the oil lamp. But there was no hoped-for stack of dusty firewood beside the low stone hearth. They turned their attention to the rest of the room and soon found another oil lamp. With both lit, they took stock of the entire space, and with each new discovery their confusion grew greater.

It appeared to be an old, abandoned home of some sort. Maybe a stage stop? But not out here—in the midst of untouched ranchland where whites had been settled but half a man's lifetime. As they stepped slowly through the dusty, long room their lamplight revealed items familiar to them: poker tables with chips and cards played on top, glasses and bottles beside them on the baize surfaces. Ranged along the far back wall was a well-built bar, just the right height for a man to lean on while he drank. Behind it along the wall stood bottles webbed with dust and the debris of a long-forgotten place. Above them on the wall were paintings of bawdy-house women reclining and beckoning, their scantily clad bodies pocked with dust and sagging with cobwebs.

Finally Rigby spoke in a low, hoarse whisper. "You ever heard tell of a saloon in these parts, Horton?"

"No, no way. But look, right now it is what it is, and we need to bust up some of this furniture and get warm. Then we can investigate."

They set to smashing up a couple of straight-back chairs and a gaming table, its baize top emitting a cloud of dust as they struck it down and cleaved the surface with their stomping boots. In short minutes they had a decent fire roaring in the fireplace, and a few more chairs and another table fell prey to their hunger for heat.

Soon, scant heat soaked into their limbs and reddened their faces as they bent low, too close to the licking flames, their backs to the dark saloon.

"Hey! Hey!"

Both men jumped and spun to face the room. Only their hard breathing and the crackle of fire eating wood behind them could be heard.

"You heard that voice, right?" said Rigby, not looking away from the dark gloom of the room before him.

"Yeah, yeah I did."

He scarcely got the words out when a man's brittle laugh, as if heard from the far end of a long hallway, reached them.

"Draw your six-gun. We can't let someone pull the wool on us."

The younger man nodded, swallowed dryly.

With their lamps in one hand and drawn and cocked pistols in the other, the two men advanced toward the far end of the structure, toward the bar, the roaring fire they had built offering them slight confidence as the temperature in the room slowly rose.

"It come from back there, behind the bar, I think."

"I thought it came from that back corner—I'll check there." Rigby step-stopped, step-stopped his way over, seeing nothing but long shadows as he advanced on yet another dusty table and two chairs. Then he heard Horton gasp and moan. "What's wrong?" He bolted back to the older man's side.

Horton nodded toward the bar, indicating something unseen just behind it. "Saw a man, a barkeep. He was bald, in his shirtsleeves. Smiled at me, then he was gone." Horton turned to the younger man. "Just like that—gone!"

"Someone's having fun with us."

The fire cracked and popped and low sounds began to increase all around them, odd sounds as if heard through the walls of an adjoining room. The men exchanged glances and walked backward toward the fire. From behind them they heard the unmistakable clink of poker chips hitting others, then a woman giggled. No matter how fast they spun, looking in the direction of each new noise, they saw nothing but the same old dusty room filled with twitching, stretched shadows. Then they both smelled cigar smoke, though none hung in the air.

They made it back to the fireplace and piled on more bits of broken chairs and tables. And as the room heated up, the sounds of a saloon in full swing on a busy night grew louder and louder all around them. The two worn-out cowboys stared at each other in terror, their eyes wider than possible, their frostbitten cheeks drawn tight, their teeth rigid behind the grim set of their mouths. They didn't dare speak. Each seemed to know without telling the other that they had to stay the night in this hellish scene come to life in this building that shouldn't even be there, had to stick it out or risk sure death in the storm, still raging around them just outside.

All night long the cowboys stood there, inching away from the fire only to fetch chairs, old crates, anything that might burn, dragging it back before them. With the fire to their backs, the room's diminishing supply of furniture formed a dusty bulwark against the boisterous unseen crowd before them.

Whenever one of them dared to speak, voices would laugh, words would be said, unintelligible words, but more of the same spoken in conversation all around them. All night long.

Untold hours seemed to pass before they saw the raw light of early dawn slipping through cracks in the doorway. The new day had also brought an easing of the storm, for no snow blew in the crack left by the ill-fitting door. Had it been only one night? It seemed to them a lifetime ago.

Without a word to each other, they made for the door, trying to not turn their backs on the room. As soon as they squeezed through the doorway they made their way around the outside of the building to the lean-to. And inside stood their horses, looking, if not happy, at least alive and fidgety. The men led them out, looked to the mountains in the distance for direction, and busted trail for a few dozen yards before mounting up.

Long minutes passed before they could even look at each other, incredulity and helplessness writ large on their faces. It was Horton who spoke, in a hoarse whisper, what they each had been thinking. "I don't know what went on back there, but I'll tell you what—I ain't spending another minute of my life anywhere on this here range. I'd rather die tramping in any direction than stay in these parts another second."

"I'm with you, pard. Let's git gone."

And the men rode, the cold sun doing little to help them. But they kept on, their mounts punching holes in snowdrifts. And on the second day they came within sight of a line shack familiar to them.

The cowboys waiting for them were from the home ranch. They'd been sent out to check on Horton and Rigby. The blizzard's intensity had spooked the foreman and he wanted to make sure his men—and beeves—were alive. The men, it seemed, were, but many cattle had been lost.

The two men were nursed back to health at the home ranch, but they could not be convinced to alter their plans. Within the week they left the employ of the ranch and rode off together for another range, vowing to never set foot in Park County, Wyoming, ever again.

The frightening ordeal the two cowboys underwent that frigid winter night in the last decades of the nineteenth century has remained one of the most oft-repeated legends among the many ranches that still populate the windswept rangelands of the West. To their ends, the two men vowed that what they experienced was the truth.

If you should be interested in finding the phantom saloon for yourself, remember that all you really need to do is become hopelessly lost on horseback in a blizzard in the middle of Park County, Wyoming. And just maybe you'll find an old shack that shouldn't exist and that may or may not house spirits that will scare the dickens out of you. But remember that two cowboys swore it happened to them. And a cowboy never lies.

Chapter 16
The Bloody St. James

St. James Hotel
Cimarron, New Mexico

Twenty-six men were killed in gunfights within the walls of Lambert's Place (now the St. James Hotel). The saloon sports four hundred bullet holes in the ceiling. Guests included Clay Allison, Black Jack Ketchum, Jesse James, Buffalo Bill Cody, Bat Masterson, Pat Garrett, Wyatt Earp. . . . At this hotel—still popular with both the living and the dead—the second floor has cold spots, unseen hands, cigar smoke, and cowboys in mirrors, and Room 18 must be kept locked because of the ill-tempered spirit within. Room 17 is inhabited by a woman who taps at her window, and "the Little Imp," a dwarflike ghost, plays tricks on staff. It would seem the Bloody St. James is haunted.

On the night of March 31, 1882, Thomas James Wright, T.J. to his friends, had just had a fine meal in the dining room of the St. James Hotel, and he had intended to linger in the saloon for a while, sipping whiskey, trying to convince himself to call it an early night. Problem was, he wasn't all that tired. What he really wanted was a little time with a woman, but he knew that the owner's wife, Mary Lambert, frowned on bringing in the doves, at least until she went to bed. Then the ladies would sneak in a side door. That suited him right down to the ground. But what to do until then?

A man next to him finished off a mug of beer and dragged a shirt cuff across his moustache. The barkeep asked if he wanted another.

"Nope, better not. I got to be sharp for the game."

The bartender nodded and scooped up the empty beer glass.

Wright looked at the man beside him. "You say there's going to be a poker game?" He scanned the room but didn't see any dealings going on.

The fat man eyed him, then motioned with his head toward the room's interior exit. "Upstairs, game going on right now. I'm headed there myself. I guess you'd be welcome—but you got to have money to get in on it."

Wright bristled a little at this and stood up straight. "Don't you worry about that. My money's good. You just lead the way."

"All right then, come on."

Short minutes later found the two men seated at the baize table upstairs, nodding to the other gathered men. "Ten dollars to get in," said one, a scowling fellow with a thick cigar poking from the center of his mouth.

Wright didn't want to appear unsuited to the task, so he merely nodded and joined in the game, silently making quick mental calculations that would tell him how long he could play without jeopardizing his bankroll.

But a few hours later found T.J. Wright raking in yet another pile of winnings. And he silently thanked his lucky stars he hadn't had too much to drink; otherwise he might not have won all those hands. This was a substantial haul and he knew it wouldn't last. "Gents, I aim to call it a night. I'm done and I thank you all for a most pleasurable evening." He laid out $10 and said, "Drinks on me, boys."

But the surly man with the cigar trembled in rage, his teeth set tight together, the cigar long extinguished and gripped in his left hand. "You ain't even going to give us a chance to win back what you stole?"

Wright stood up, eased back his frock coat so that his six-gun was visible, and said, "I stole nothing." He stared hard at the man. "But I won a whole lot." With that, Wright smiled and, stuffing the rest of his winnings into his pocket, he left the cards room and headed down the hall to his room, number 18.

He would have a drink in his room and call it a night. As he walked down the hall, hurried footsteps sounded behind him. Before he could turn, he heard a pistol's hammer ratcheting back into the deadliest position of all. Then deafening sound and smoke accompanied a pummeling force, as if someone had rammed into his back with the butt end of a log and drove him to his knees. He would have dropped face first to the hallway's carpet, but he reached out and braced himself against the wall.

Wadded-up cash popped free from his inside coat pocket, but he didn't care. He'd been shot in the back and it hurt like hell. He was having trouble breathing, and his vision wavered. He wanted a cool glass of water; he wanted more than anything to be in his own bed, back home, miles from there. But he'd settle for the bed just a few feet away in his room. There it was, before him, the door to his room. He heard a gurgling noise, like a steam valve trickling down its pent-up pressure. As he crawled forward, dragging himself along on his knees and half propped on his elbows, he realized the sound was his own breathing. He was lung shot, dead certain.

Make it to the room, he told himself. *Make it to your room, you're paid up for the night, you can stay there until you heal, then ride on out of here and never look back. Just make it to the room.*

And Thomas James Wright did make it into his room—and by the next morning, he'd bled to death in the bed.

Randy Smith poked his wife in the shoulder. "Hey, honey, you smell that?"

"Oh, for heaven's sake, Randy . . ."

"No, I smell roses. I'm serious."

His wife lay still a moment, then whispered, "Me, too. You think it's her?"

"Must be," he whispered. "You scared?"

Again, his wife was silent for a few moments, then said, "No, not really. Just the same, don't do anything to make her mad."

"What do you think I'm going to do?" Though it was a hot night in July, he pulled the covers up under his chin. After a few minutes, he said, "It's really perfumey."

His wife sighed. "Well, open a window then."

"You're closer. . . ."

"Oh, for heaven's sake," she said again as she heaved herself out of bed. She opened the window a few inches and a cool draft of night air wafted in. "Satisfied?" she said, climbing back into bed. She turned over and fell asleep.

It took Randy awhile longer, but then he, too, dozed off, the cloying smell of roses mostly gone.

It was a sound that woke Randy next. A tapping noise . . . as if someone were tapping fingernails on the window. Impossible, as they were in an upstairs room. But it didn't stop. And it definitely seemed to be coming from the window. This time he did not need to wake his wife. The tapping did that for him.

"Randy, what is that?"

"It's . . . someone tapping on the window."

She sat upright. "Oh God," she whispered. "It's definitely her."

"Mrs. What's-her-name? The old owner of the place?"

"Mary Lambert, yeah. Remember I told you about the smell of roses in this room, Room 17?"

"Yeah," he whispered, knowing he would hate what he was about to hear.

"Well, when you were getting our bags out of the car, they also told me that you can't open the window, or she'll tap on it until you close it. I sort of forgot until now."

"Oh," he said, really regretting letting his wife talk him into staying in a haunted hotel room.

They stared at each other in the dark, the smell of roses all around them and the insistent, unceasing tapping sound emanating from the glass of the open window.

"Your turn," said Randy's wife, lying down and pulling the covers over her head.

The sound of a man's unintelligible yelling voice woke nearly everyone in the St. James Hotel on that last night of March, several decades ago. The angry voice repeated a series of odd, raging oaths, the tone of which grew increasingly frenzied. He followed it up with pounding that rattled a door that apparently refused to open. From behind their own doors, guests listened as his bellowed shouts became higher pitched, his pounding more emphatic, his shouts turning to screams, and then they heard a crash followed by a long silence. The sounds had come from the end of the hall, down by the two most haunted rooms in the place. Finally they heard low voices and the jangling keys of what must have been hotel employees in the hallway.

When the keys one after the other refused to work the lock, and the knob refused to budge in either direction, a manager's voice could be heard berating someone, his clipped, harsh tone growing angry: "Why did you rent out this room? What did I tell you about Room 18? He doesn't like to be disturbed!"

"But I didn't rent this room, sir. No one did. . . . "

The manager squinted at the clerk. "Then it's him." He sighed. "Still, I should check inside." But still he hesitated.

They heard the voices of guests whispering in nearby rooms.

"Everything's quiet now, sir. Maybe we should try it one more time."

The manager's voice grunted in agreement and the keys jangled and rattled against the door. They heard the sound of the padlock, then the door lock clicking, the mechanism releasing. The door swung inward.

No one was in the room. In the dim glow of the manager's flashlight beam, he saw the bed with no mattress, the rocking chair, and on the bureau top, the customary half-filled bottle of whiskey, a drinking glass, and a deck of playing cards. He also smelled cigar smoke, and though there was no smoking in the hotel, this was one guest he'd long ago decided not to reprimand.

The manager backed toward the doorway, and just before he stepped into the hallway, he felt a hand push him backward square in the chest. He staggered into the clerk, who held him upright. He hastily shut the door, and with shaking hands locked the old mechanism and the newer padlock. As they walked down the hallway, the manager turned to the clerk. "What's today's date?"

"It's, um, March 31, at least for another hour. Why?"

The manager nodded. "Because Mr. Wright, permanent resident of Room 18, was killed here on this night in 1882."

The clerk's eyes grew wide. "I need a drink."

"Good idea," said the manager, rubbing his chest.

They both headed downstairs to toast the spirit of Thomas James Wright.

Tempted by the allure of gold, Henri Lambert, personal chef to President Abraham Lincoln, decided after his employer's murder to relocate out west. Having little luck finding gold, Lambert was soon enticed by businessmen in Cimarron, New Mexico. He and his wife built what was called Lambert's Place in 1872.

Cimarron (Spanish for "wild") was indeed a raucous place, sited as it was on the busy Santa Fe Trail, and much of the rowdiness took place at Lambert's. This untethered behavior led to twenty-six documented killings on the premises, not surprising considering the regularity with which drunken cowboys shot at the ceiling—roughly four hundred bullet holes have been found in the ceiling above the old bar (now the hotel's dining room), twenty-two of which are still visible in the pressed tin ceiling.

Despite such antics, the Lamberts' business thrived and in 1880 they added on, making the place into a proper hotel. It was considered one of the finest west of the Mississippi River—and one of the first to offer running water to its guests. And what a guest list it was: Jesse James, Black Jack Ketchum, Buffalo Bill Cody, Bat Masterson, Pat Garrett, Wyatt Earp, Lew Wallace, Zane Grey—and many other notable Old West names. Notorious killer Clay Allison danced nude atop the bar on at least one occasion when he'd had a snootful.

It has been speculated, but not proven, that the twenty-two-year-old gambler, Thomas James Wright, permanent resident of Room 18 (still not rented out to guests, by the way), won ownership of the hotel on that fateful night in 1882. Though little has been said of Henri Lambert's involvement, he surely would have been the number-one suspect. Perhaps Cimarron's lawless ways worked in his favor.

Through a succession of owners in the twentieth century, and a name change to the St. James Hotel, what was once one of the most famous—and infamous—saloons and hotels in the West fell into disrepair. In 1985 the hotel came under new ownership and was brought back to its original, impressive state. In 1988 a ten-room annex with modern conveniences was added.

In addition to the angry ghost of T.J. Wright, the St. James is also home to the ghost of Mary Lambert, who died in 1926 and delicately haunts Room 17, her old room. And then there's the homely, dwarflike mischievous spirit called "the Little Imp" by staff. The devilish shade regularly pushes dishes off counters and "relocates" small items around the hotel.

Most of the hauntings take place on the second floor of the hotel, though the visage of a cowboy has appeared several times in the mirror behind the bar downstairs, staring back at whoever is looking into the glass. Yet when people spin around, he's not there.

Chapter 17

Ghost Bride of
the Golden North

Golden North Hotel
Skagway, Alaska

*Though closed as a place of accommodation since 2002, Skagway's
Golden North Hotel was Alaska's oldest hotel. It was built in 1898 and
moved to its present location in 1908. A third floor was added, along
with its famous golden dome. The building is said to be the haunt of
two entities, one of which, Mary, inhabits Room 23. The tragic figure
checked into the hotel in 1898, expecting her fiancé to return soon
from the gold fields of the Klondike. Poor Mary waited in vain, fell ill
with pneumonia, wasted away, and died in the hotel. But she did not
leave. And neither did the entity in Room 14.*

"I expect he'll be back within a few weeks, maybe a month
or two." The pretty young woman named Mary gazed out
the dining room window of the Golden North Hotel, a slight
smile on her face as she thought of her fiancé, battling the
elements as he scooped up nuggets of gold from the stream-
beds of the Klondike. At least that was how she had pictured
it when he told her how it would be.

The florid older woman in the bright blue dress, with
whom Mary shared her breakfast table, shook her head and
buttered another wedge of cornbread. "You are fooling yourself, dearie. That man ain't going to find enough gold to put
in your eye. And what's more, if he gets back in a year, you'll

be lucky. Why, first he has to leg it on over White Pass to Bennett Lake, then he has to float five hundred miles on the Yukon River to Dawson City." She paused to see if the young woman was listening to her.

Mary looked at the untouched food on her own plate, her smile fading.

The big woman took a bite of cornbread. After a few moments of vigorous chewing, she said, "I don't mean to scare you, but you're just not being realistic." She turned and faced the girl. "You ought to go back to where you came from, wait for him there. Better yet, find yourself a young man who doesn't have the gold fever. It'll only lead to heartbreak."

Mary stood, her face tight, trembling, and on the brink of tears. "What do you know about him? About us? About any of this?" She waved an arm at the window.

The big woman smiled. "I understand you're a little raw after hearing what I said. But I'll tell you what, missy. I have more experience of this place than you will ever get, God willin'."

"What do you mean?"

"I mean that I lost my man to the lousy lure of gold in the Klondike. That was two years ago. And now I'm working as a madam. Who knew that was in the cards for me?" She laughed and slapped the tabletop. "Only thing I could do that I damn sure knew I could do."

There was a lull in the conversation and Mary set her napkin down on her plate. "I'm sorry, I didn't mean . . ."

"Pish posh, girl. I don't need your pity. Only thing I want from you is to rethink your plans. And if you end up needing money to get back home, wherever that may be, you just come see me. I'm at the Red Onion, upstairs. Pretty pale flower like you, I bet we can work out some way for you to earn a little traveling cash." She winked.

Mary put a hand to her mouth and fled the dining room. Later, in her room, she wept as she stared out the window. Could what that horrid woman said be true? Surely her dear fiancé wouldn't lie to her. He would come back soon. He had to—what would she do? How would she survive in this forsaken town? Oh, all this worry left her so very tired.

She'd felt this way for days now, and had begun coughing, too. But she couldn't spend her money on a doctor, not that one of any repute could be found in such a town. She told herself all she really needed to do was rest and wait for it to pass.

Mary wet a washcloth from the basin on the dresser, climbed into the bed, and laid the cloth on her hot forehead. She sighed, not at all sure of anything now—not her fiancé and his promised good fortune, not his safe return, not her own increasingly fragile health. *Soon,* thought Mary, *soon I shall leave this place. Just as soon as he returns for me.*

The soft sound, like the fluttering wings of a moth, woke Willard Flattery. Where was he? Oh yes. Skagway, Alaska. The Golden North Hotel. *What a pretty building,* he remembered thinking as he drove up. He'd promised himself he would stay at the hotel on his next business trip to Skagway after he found out that it was the oldest hotel in Alaska. It had taken longer than he expected, but he finally made it to the bustling town, and he was glad he did.

But what was that sound? There it was again . . . fluttering. A bat? Had a bat gotten into his room? Pay good money at a hotel, you should at least expect to not have bats in your room. He'd be sure someone heard about it in the morning . . . but wait, that wasn't it. He reached for the bedside lamp, but there was the sound again. Not a bat's wings, more drawn out, like soft fabric, rippling, sliding over itself as if in a breeze. Where?

His eyes picked out something by the window. A woman in a dress, as if lit from within, the collar high on her thin neck. She wore an old-time hairstyle, pulled back, and she looked out the window. Now she turned and stared at him. What looked like tendrils of living smoke curled from her mouth and her shoulders, and though she seemed to be standing, her body ended just below her waist, where it vaporized in the dark night air of the room. A sudden wash of coldness passed through him, and then she appeared in eye-blink speed beside the bed.

She leaned over him, closer, closer, her arms outstretched, hands with fingers that seemed to float and waver, reaching for him, toward his face, a calm, confused look on her gauzy features. He tried to raise his arms, to push the thing away, but they wouldn't work, and he couldn't make them rise from the covers.

Her hands never touched him, but Willard felt his throat tighten as if fingers were closing over his windpipe, tighter, tighter. . . . Even as he screamed, forcing sound through his constricting throat, it felt to Willard as if he were about to expire from some great, raging fever. He longed for a cool drink, something to open his throat, something to help him breathe again.

The scream, when it finally came, was a ragged, hoarse sound that ripped from his throat as if pulled by a hand. Before his wide-open eyes, the floating woman faded from sight and was gone, and the fevered, gasping feeling was soon replaced with the cool, fresh air flowing through the window screen.

And he was left to explain to the people pounding on his door why he had screamed.

A week after a young couple returned home to Solon, Ohio, from their trip to Alaska, they picked up their developed film at the drug store. In the picture the young lady had taken of her boyfriend in the hallway of the third floor of the Golden North Hotel, a young woman in a white dress was standing beside him. She did not look terribly happy or healthy. In fact, she looked a bit pale. She also had not been there when the picture was taken.

In 1887, in anticipation of the region's opening up to gold seekers, a man named Captain William "Billy" Moore, along with his son, Ben, established a foothold along the Yukon River and built a homestead, a pier, and a sawmill. Gold was discovered nearby, and within a year the raw outpost became Skagway, which soon blossomed to a bustling burg of ten thousand gold-minded souls.

Though the precious metal would be discovered in copious quantities far inland (giving birth to such mine camps as Dawson City, which reached a population of thirty thousand by 1898), Skagway became an important jumping-off point for the thousands of Argonauts heading inland to the gold fields of the Klondike. Skagway's role became that of a thriving center of commerce, home to many businesses catering to their rapacious and burgeoning needs.

One of those businesses, a new two-story building that housed the Klondike Trading Company, did a brisk business, but not for long. The gold supply appeared to be dwindling, and the demand for supplies with it. Skagway's population quickly followed suit. The building became an army barracks, and then in 1909 it was moved from Third and State Streets to Third and Broadway Streets, where a third story and its famed golden dome were added. And it was reborn as the Golden North Hotel, the second structure in Skagway to be thus named.

The first no longer exists, having been torn down once the gold rush came to an end. But curiously, it is that first Golden North Hotel in which poor Mary waited in vain for her fiancé to return from finding his fortune in the Klondike. And it is in that first hotel she died. But when the newer incarnation, complete with the same name and same owners, was established, Mary's ghost found a new home. It apparently offered enough similarities that the distraught ghost was able to settle in for the duration.

The (new) Golden North Hotel remained a place of accommodation for nearly a century before closing in 2002. The downstairs space has been reworked to accommodate a number of shops and an eatery. But Room 23 has been left as it was when the hotel was open for business, perhaps allowing Mary a place to continue to hang her hat. Alas, she's been denied further chances to choke overnight guests, especially those who remind her of the fiancé who never returned from the gold fields.

And Room 14 is the home of another entity. This one, a light form of some sort, has been witnessed, caught in photographs, and filmed numerous times, day and night. Harmless, it appears to be content with playfully darting about the room.

Skagway is also home to several other haunted hotspots, including the City Municipal Building, where odd noises emanating from the second floor have been heard for decades. The second floor of Eagles Hall is home to what have been called friendly ghosts, though a creeping cold feeling and strange noises have caused people to flee the building. Mulvihill House is said to still be home to Mul Mulvihill, who in life was dispatcher for the famed White Pass and Yukon Railroad. His heavy tread walking upstairs and the jarring *clackety-clack* of his telegraph key can still be heard throughout the house.

The Red Onion Saloon was once a bordello, and a prostitute's shadowy ghost can be seen watering nonexistent plants. The dove's perfume wafts through the hallways and her footsteps can also be heard at odd times. And nearby, the deserted White House was, among other things, a day-care center. The ghost of the woman who ran it has been seen staring out the windows of the deserted husk of a building, wondering, perhaps, where all the children have gone.

Part Four

PRISON, FORT & BATTLEFIELD

Chapter 18

The Unliving Hell
of Yuma Prison

Yuma Territorial Prison State Historic Park
Yuma, Arizona

Killers, thieves, rapists, flim-flam artists, gamblers, drunks—Arizona's famed Yuma Territorial Prison was home to more than 3,069 hard cases, men and women, through the years. And 111 of them died within the bleak stone walls of their cells. Badman John Ryan hung himself in Cell 14, and now his ghost paces a groove in the hard stone floor of that same cell. Many people who have seen him report feeling a distinct drop in the surrounding air temperature. They also see, for a few seconds, his eyes as shining lights, his body a faint white glow. And Ryan is but one of the spooks to haunt the decaying old prison ruin.

The Yuma Territorial Prison volunteer attendant stood beside the locked strap-steel door to one of the cells and scanned the milling visitors. *It's always the same,* she thought, *slowpokes and stragglers who can't seem to help stopping and staring into the deep, dark recesses of the bleak cells.* But she couldn't blame them. It was all too easy to imagine oneself locked in, no hope of parole, in the sweltering steel-and-stone prison. The place could get downright creepy at times, especially as the sun began its downward arc for the day.

A sudden scream split the air. The jarring sound brought everyone's head around, and the musing attendant knew even before she looked just where it would be coming from. Her eyes locked on a twenty-something woman who had dropped her handbag and, hands to her mouth, was backing away from the locked door of Cell 14. John Ryan's cell. The attendant rushed to the young woman's aid as other visitors closed in.

"It's okay, folks. Give her some room. Miss, are you all right? Miss?"

The young woman was breathing heavily and had begun to cry. "In that cell, I saw . . ."

"What did you see?"

She finally looked away from the cell door.

"You can tell me," said the attendant. "I guarantee I've heard it before. That cell is haunted."

The young woman appeared relieved. Someone brought her handbag to her and she rummaged for a hankie. "I was just looking into the cell, even though it's rather dark and looks about like all the rest. I was ready to turn away, but then I thought I heard a scuffing sound. I gripped the flat steel bars and looked through one of the squares. And that's when I saw it."

"What was that, ma'am?" the attendant asked.

"I saw the faint outline of a man." She looked around quickly at the small throng of other visitors. "I swear it. He was thin but vaporous. It was more like a shadow of a man. I was barely able to make him out. He was pacing back and forth, back and forth in there, and it seemed as if he was muttering to himself. I know how crazy this sounds, but I swear it's true. It was hypnotizing. But then he looked up at me and his eyes were bright red like fiery coals, and he made a hideous growling sound and . . ." She began to shake again. "Oh, it was terrible. He came at me, I swear it! He lunged at me!"

But no one laughed. Instead they began to ask questions and several moved toward Cell 14 as the attendant explained John Ryan's unnerving story.

"You quit that pacing, else you gonna work a groove in that stone floor."

The man in Cell 14 looked at the guard, a growling sound rising from his throat, then shook his head and kept pacing.

"Should have left you in with them other foul creatures," snarled the guard. "I have no doubt that you will rot in hell when your time comes. I will probably be there at some point myself. Difference is I never did commit no crime like you did. Boss man says you're in here for what they call a 'crime against nature.' I would guess that in hell, that makes all the difference."

"Sounds like you know what you talk of," said the prisoner, John Ryan. "Could be I'll put a good word in for you when I get there."

"Yeah, you do that."

"Why don't you go away now and leave a man to himself."

"You foul scum. How dare you talk to me like that? I am a guard and you ain't nothing but a prisoner."

John Ryan kept pacing, but the guard could see that he'd gotten to him, could see the prisoner's jaw muscles working, bunching and unbunching as if he were chewing something. He saw the veins in the man's temple stand out and pulse. Saw Ryan's hands clench and unclench as if he wanted to reach out and strangle something.

It was just like the other guard said—you keep annoying him and Ryan will eventually lose control, start screaming and shouting, swearing, spitting, and when he gets that way, you can throw him in the Dark Cell for a few days, let him cool off. The guard reckoned that he could have left well enough alone, but he'd been here a month and hadn't had the chance himself to escort any prisoners to the Dark Cell, something he was looking forward to. 'Course, with a prisoner like Ryan, you had to have help. He was ornery and tricky, no telling what the rascal could get up to.

"Ain't nobody in here likes you, Ryan. I suspect strongly that it's the case on the outside, too. Why, I hear tell you have children and a pretty little wife somewheres. Might be I'll look her up. It ain't like you'll be seeing her anytime soon."

That's all it took. From his favored pacing spot at the rear of the cell, Ryan launched himself toward the strap-steel cell door. Snarling like a dog, he grasped at the guard through the square holes in the door. Spittle dripped off his chin as he howled and raged, filling the air with a blue streak of foul language that froze everyone in earshot.

Soon enough, other prisoners began shouting and laughing at Ryan, the most reviled of prisoners. He was one of the few who had been placed in a cell all by himself, so disliked was he. The warden was afraid the other inmates would gang up on Ryan and beat him to death. And he didn't want such a black mark on his record.

Three other guards showed up at Ryan's cell door and entered, a shotgun held to the back of Ryan's head. "You know the drill, Ryan," said the most senior of the guards. "Shuck them duds down to your underwear."

"No, sir. I ain't going to the Dark Cell again. Ain't doin' it."

The guard cocked the hammer on the scattergun and said nothing. But he could see in Ryan's eyes that he'd already given up, resigned himself to the fact that he soon would be in the dank hole again.

"Must be you're getting used to it."

Ryan walked past the rows of cell doors, under his heavy escort, past the hoots and jeers of other prisoners, his chains swinging from his manacled arms, and dragging in the dirt as he shuffled forward. He acted as if didn't hear them, and remained quiet, walking a bit slower as they unlocked the steel door that led to the long, dark corridor hewn from rock into the cliff face. The guards swung a second door and nudged him forward to the center of the near-black space, where they secured his chain to the ring in the floor of the Dark Cell. As they reached the door to leave him there, in a quieter voice than he'd used in days, he said, "I ain't eaten yet."

The guards stopped, sighed. "You know the rules at Yuma Prison as well as I do, Ryan. You get fed once a day here in the hole. Bread and water once a day."

The guard swung the door wide, stepped through, and as it squawked shut, said, "I do believe you missed the kitchen call. Now you just gonna have to wait until tomorrow to get your rations." He locked the door, his heavy keys clanking dully against each other, his laughter echoing throughout the bleak chamber.

Ryan was, in a small way, grateful for the seclusion, sealed off in the black cavern, away from the taunts and jeers of guards and fellow prisoners. But he knew that soon the scorpions and snakes would creep in, dropped down the rocky ventilation shaft by the guards. It had happened plenty of times in the past. He wondered how long he would be in the Dark Cell this time. Seemed to get longer each time. Ryan did his best to pace, but his mobility was limited, chained as he was to the steel ring in the floor.

That was in November. By the end of March 1903, John Ryan was dead, found swinging in his cell, a crude but effective rope made of his own blankets cinched tight about his neck. Though his body was buried in the prison graveyard, he never really left Cell 14, where he'd spent so much time pacing back and forth, back and forth, wearing a polished path in the stone floor.

If ever there was a place tailor-made for a ghost to dwell, it is Yuma Territorial Prison. Called Hell Hole and Devil's Island by inmates and local residents, the prison was ideally sited in the midst of an unforgiving landscape, high on a rocky knob from where guards could see for miles in all directions. On July 1, 1876, the jail opened by closing its doors on its first seven inmates. They also happened to be the prisoners who built it on hard rock cliffs close by the Gila and Colorado Rivers, with the town of Yuma off to the west. Over the years inmates ranged in age from fourteen to eighty-eight, men and women, Apache, Europeans, Mexicans, Americans—all did their time between 1876 and 1909.

Residents of nearby Yuma called the prison a country club. It was outfitted with electricity as early as 1885, with blowers that fed cool air into the sweltering stone cells. The facility had a modern hospital, a library with educational facilities, language and music classes, and a band.

But at night it was six men to a narrow stone cell. They shared a slop bucket for their toilet necessities, and baths were provided once a week. The cells stank of body odor and slops, and crawled with lice, bedbugs, roaches, snakes, and scorpions. Disease, rape, and murder were part of life at Yuma Prison. Anyone who broke prison rules (refusing to bathe, swearing, fighting, making weapons) would be forced to wear a ball and chain. If he continued in his roguish ways, the prisoner could expect to spend lengthy terms of severe isolation in the Dark Cell: a long, dark passageway dug into a hillside that ended in a fifteen-by-fifteen-foot windowless cell where he would be chained from one to twelve days. One prisoner, John Clay, spent 104 days straight in the Dark Cell, after which he was reported to be a model prisoner. Other prisoners did not emerge from the Dark Cell so well and were transferred to the insane asylum in Phoenix. Most of the prison's 3,069 inmates served their time and were released, 26 escaped (of 140 attempts), and 111 prisoners died within the walls at Yuma Prison, 104 of whom are buried in the prison cemetery.

Eventually the prison became overcrowded and unfit for housing inmates. By mid-September 1909, the last convict was transported to the new prisoner-built territorial facility in Florence, Arizona. In the ensuing years, Yuma Prison became the local high school, a homeless shelter during the Depression, a movie set, and over the years floods, thieves, and the ever-expanding railroads and highways all claimed portions of the sprawling complex. But local residents saw potential for preservation of this historic hotel for hostiles, and by 1941 they had spiffed up the place and opened a museum on site. Two decades later, in 1961, it became the third of Arizona's official state parks.

Visitors who venture down the long, bleak walk to the heart of the Dark Cell—and who happen to be wearing red— are frequently pinched, yelled at, and otherwise harassed by the ghost of a little girl. The ghost of an inmate showed up in the background of a tourist's photo from the 1930s, and a playful spirit dwells in the museum and gift shop, and is frequently caught fondling dimes in the cash register.

Several years ago, a magazine writer vowed to spend the night chained in the Dark Cell. She lasted only a few hours before begging to be let out—she found she was not alone in the cell.

Chapter 19

Restless at
Reno Crossing

Little Bighorn Battlefield National Monument
Crow Agency, Montana

Lieutenant Colonel George Armstrong Custer and his men were wiped out at the Battle of the Little Bighorn in June 1876. Five miles distant, Major Marcus Reno's men were forced to make a ragged retreat, dragging their dying behind them, back across the river. That spot, now known as Reno Crossing, is alive with spirits that still tread the bloodied battlegrounds. Visitors find it a cold and depressing place. The ghosts of the dead appear there, confused, lonely, and restless.

To Second Lieutenant Benjamin Hodgson, it seemed as if the Sioux and Cheyenne redoubled their efforts and their numbers with every minute that passed. And so, Major Reno had given the order to head back across the river to gain high ground. The neighing of horses and crackling of gunfire, the stink of gun smoke and blood, the screaming of men—whites and Indians—the thud of bodies hitting the muddied earth slick with human gore, it all circled Hodgson like bees on a hot summer day.

They'd just thundered into the river when Hodgson felt his horse shudder and slow. The beast had been hit. It staggered and wallowed in the current, oblivious to the rage storming all about it. Hodgson saw a puckered, bloody wound in its flank. He scrambled free of the saddle and reached out, snatched hold of the stirrup of a soldier passing close by. They reached the far side, and that's when Hodgson felt the first bullet. It slammed into him, but he did not fall to the ground. He lost his grip on the stirrup strap but reached for a helping hand offered by another rider. Then another bullet hit him. He slipped in the mud and dropped as another rider offered help. But that man stiffened in the saddle and dropped, and the horse bolted. Close by, another man and horse pitched together, wheeling, a welter of legs and screams, rolling, smacking hard into the blood-slick bank down to the water's edge.

Hodgson staggered along the bank, angling toward the ravine everyone had been headed for. Once more he fell, rose, then pulled in a deep breath and turned, drew his revolver, and faced the enemy. He managed two shots.

And that's when sound and time slowed and he saw them—the bullets that would spell his end. They drove toward him like small, determined fists, like bees, and slammed into his chest, his arm, his leg. He could make no move against it, could only watch as his uniform welled blood and he felt piercing, hot pain deep inside.

Second Lieutenant Benjamin Hodgson lay stunned, the whistling, killing sounds of battle raging all about him. Thoughts of his family came to him, and then he knew no more.

Jeff Coleman was so excited to finally be at Little Bighorn Battlefield National Monument. Or more precisely, at a nearby motel. He'd taken a week off of work and had planned on visiting the battlefield tomorrow, then maybe dip down to South Dakota, see Mount Rushmore on his way back to Minnesota next week. But it was Little Bighorn that he really wanted to spend time at. He'd been looking forward to this trip for years.

That night at the motel, he had a difficult time convincing himself to put out the light and get some sleep. As a bonus, the visit should help him add his two cents' worth to his reenactment group's heated debates about the details of the infamous and controversial battle. He wanted to tour it all, including Reno Crossing, a spot he'd read about for years. And it was Reno Crossing that was on his mind as he drifted off to sleep.

In the dark, early hours of the morning, Jeff awoke, eyes fluttered wide. Something felt wrong, odd somehow. Where was he? Oh yeah, on vacation, the motel, not far from Little Bighorn Battlefield. But what was that feeling? Was someone in the room with him? Jeff sat up in bed and squinted into the dark. At the foot of the bed sat a young man in a chair. Or rather it was a sort of gauzy shape of a young man, quietly staring at Jeff.

"Who are you? What do you want?" Jeff pulled his bedding up closer to his chin, as if it might offer protection. The young man just stared at him with the saddest eyes Jeff had ever seen.

As the fogginess of sleep left him, Jeff didn't feel afraid, even when it finally occurred to him that he was seeing a ghost. And judging from the man's attire, it was obvious he was a US Army officer. And not of the twentieth century. The young man sported a large, dark-colored moustache, of the walrus type so in vogue in the nineteenth century. But most striking of all were the feelings of sorrow and foreboding the young man exuded. The very air in the dark room was charged with a gloom so complete and depressing that Jeff felt it difficult to concentrate on the presence of the apparition staring at him from the foot of the bed. After a few minutes, the figure dissolved, his eyes never once leaving Jeff's face.

Jeff stayed propped on his elbows, tangled in his bedsheets. The feeling of dread and extreme sadness also seemed to fade with the ghostly presence, but it would be long minutes before he felt hopeful again. What could it mean? Had he truly been visited by an apparition? He'd read of the hundreds of ghostly sightings in the area, in buildings at the site of the long-ago battlegrounds.

Jeff puzzled over the ghostly figure for an hour, half expecting at any moment to see the sad young man with the oppressive demeanor fade back into the chair. . . . But he didn't and Jeff eventually fell back asleep.

He awoke hours later, though still early, perplexed about his ghostly visitor but excited about the coming day. When he went downstairs for coffee and a bagel, he told the motel clerk what had happened, but made it sound like he'd had a dream. But Jeff was more convinced than ever that it had been real.

The clerk nodded. "It's happened before."

"It has?" Jeff dropped the pretense that he'd thought it a dream. "But . . . it was so depressing. Who is the ghost, do you know?"

"You're headed to the battlefield and Reno Crossing, right?"

Jeff nodded.

"I guessed as much. You'll see," said the clerk. And she wouldn't say anything more about it.

Later that day, at the Little Bighorn River location known as Reno Crossing, Jeff saw a marker by the water showing where Second Lieutenant Benjamin Hodgson had died on June 25, 1876. At the time of the battle, he was acting adjutant to Major Reno.

Later, at the visitor center, Jeff got into a conversation with the attendant and sheepishly told her what had happened to him the night before. She smiled and showed Jeff a photograph of a smart young officer.

"Is this who visited you?"

Jeff's shock was evident. "Yeah, but how. . ."

"It's happened before, many times. Apparently Hodgson likes to visit people who are headed to Reno Crossing the next day. It's almost like he's warning them of the dangers of the place."

Jeff stared at the photo. "I wonder how long he'll wander like that, so sad and restless."

"Forever, I'd guess," said the attendant.

Even before the soldiers of the Seventh Cavalry departed Fort Abraham Lincoln in North Dakota in May 1876, Custer's widow, Elizabeth Bacon Custer, described in her memoirs how as the troops proceeded out of the fort, an optical illusion was witnessed by all gathered there to bid the soldiers well. They watched as the long lines of soldiers seemed to divide, with half the men on horseback and on foot departing from the trail and climbing as if by magic into the sky before dissipating altogether in a haze of cloud and sun. In retrospect, it has been treated as a premonition of the unfortunate events to befall the Seventh Cavalry at the Battle of the Little Bighorn.

On June 25–26, 1876, 263 soldiers led by Lieutenant Colonel George A. Custer died before the gathered might of several thousand Lakota and Cheyenne warriors. Major Marcus Reno realized what was happening and made the decision to retreat across the Little Bighorn River in an effort to save lives and regain high ground. The location has become known as Reno Crossing, a place where roughly forty men died trying to get to safety.

Today the entire area that long ago made up the brutal battlefield is visited by more than a quarter-million people each year. It is a sacred place and many visitors feel a sense of deep melancholia and dread, as if whatever hopefulness they had felt before they visited seemed to vanish and a feeling of gloom that enveloped the place seemed, too, to close around them.

Three years after the battle, the site became a US National Cemetery, affording protection of the soldiers' graves. Eventually a superintendent was hired to watch over the landmark. His residence, built of stone—and appropriately called the Stone House—is well known to be haunted. Incidents inside include loud banging sounds, rapping noises, as if knuckles on wood, footsteps echoing on wood floors, and lights flickering on and off.

Doorknobs have been seen twisting rapidly, and when the doors are opened wide by the startled witness, there's no one on the other side. Perhaps the most disturbing of all is the appearance of a spectral figure that stared down at a park ranger while he was lying in his bed. The apparition turned and left the room—through the wall.

Several times throughout the intervening century and a half, Indian warriors on horseback, carrying shields and lances, and wearing feathers, have been spotted, skylined atop a bluff along the river nearby. Inspections of the location have revealed no hoof prints that might indicate mounted warriors were there.

Custer's ghost has also been spotted roaming the battle site, wearing a baffled look and in a state of obvious agitation. And back at Fort Abraham Lincoln, on the day her husband died, Elizabeth Custer is said to have fainted without warning at four p.m., the same time her husband met his end.

A number of people over the years have become lost wandering the riverbanks and fields of the battle sites. Their friends and family members have looked for them, to no avail, and yet they turn up, confused, exhausted, and frightened. They say that they wandered into the very battle, with all the mayhem and bloodshed raging about them. And just before their friends from the present find them, the entire battle scene vanishes and they find themselves back in the present, their lives forever changed.

Chapter 20
Spirits of the Alamo

The Alamo
San Antonio, Texas

It seems that the brutal defeat of the Texans at the hands of Generalis-
simo Santa Anna at the Alamo in 1836 was not really their end. Many
of the hopelessly outnumbered men who lost their lives defending
the fort have since reappeared about the place, their spirits defend-
ing it with burning swords. One soldier's ghost has been spotted
numerous times striding the ramparts, as if in heavy thought. Visitors
to the Alamo also experience moans, cold spots, hissing whispers,
the marching of feet, and the wailing of the near-dead.

The soldiers worked their way back to General Juan Jose
Andrade's camp some miles from where the battle at the
Alamo took place. The general had dared not camp closer,
as the mounting stink of death and disease from the rotting
corpses meant sure death for his men. And with General
Santa Anna depending on him to maintain control of the
upstart Texan rebels, Andrade could afford no losses. He had
one thousand men to do the job, but they had not counted
on Santa Anna's capture by that damnable Sam Houston at
San Jacinto. And so, in his anger, Santa Anna had sent word
to General Andrade to raze the ravaged Alamo, a last punishment and reminder to all that General Santa Anna was not a
man to be trifled with.

But here were the men Andrade had sent to the
defeated Alamo, returning far sooner than they should

have, some of them running, some pushing their fellows out of the way, desperate to get back to the safety of his camp. But why?

General Andrade waited until these men had assembled before him, rather raggedly, he noticed, then he approached their commanding officer, Colonel Sanchez, whom Andrade had personally assigned the task of burning the Alamo to the ground.

"What is the meaning of this, Colonel? I assume you have not done as I have asked. You have returned far too soon." He shifted his gaze theatrically over the heads of his men and looked toward the Alamo. "I do not see the sky angry with flames. Why is that, I wonder?"

Sanchez, out of breath even though he had been on horseback, was trying desperately to control his breathing.

Andrade stood silently before him until the man was forced to look up at him, into his eyes. The general merely raised a questioning eyebrow.

Colonel Sanchez swallowed and in a small voice said, *"Diablos."*

"Pardon me? I must have mistaken what you said."

"Diablos, sir." The man spoke in a louder voice and tried to meet his general's hard gaze.

"Ahh, diablos. *Si,* I understand now. Well, if that is all there is to it, then by all means I am glad to hear you have disobeyed my orders."

"Sir, we have a good reason, why we were unable to burn the mission."

"I am waiting."

Sanchez licked his lips and said, "We arrived prepared to do exactly as your orders dictated. But . . ."

"But?"

"When we approached the front doors of the Alamo, as if by black magic, before our very eyes six ghosts, *diablos*, I tell you," Sanchez's speech became more animated, and his eyes grew wide and white. "They appeared as if from nowhere at all, standing before the doors of the Alamo. They were tall and thin and they shook as if by their very anger. They were clearly the spirits of the Texan soldiers, sir. And each held high a flaming sword blazing in the night sky, the flames leaping to the heavens."

"Oh?" Andrade nodded and narrowed his eyes. He really wanted to laugh at the colonel's face, but something stopped him. Never had Sanchez let him down in the past. He had been dependable until now, and the men under his command were more of the same, reliable soldiers. And yet, here they were, telling him a . . . ghost story?

"Go on, Sanchez. I have not heard a good fireside tale in a long, long time."

"But sir, I assure you, it is true. We saw it." Sanchez turned to look at the men who had accompanied him, and they all nodded vigorously.

"Sir," continued Sanchez, "the spirits howled at us, told us that we were not to harm the Alamo. 'Do not touch her walls!' they screamed. The very sockets of their eyes were black as the devil's night, their cheeks sunken, their feet did not touch the ground, but seemed to float above it. They were tall and moved as if they were made of thick smoke, and yet I swear to you, sir, they were men, or rather the deviled spirits of dead men. I swear this is true."

For a long minute, General Andrade stared at Colonel Sanchez, a man he thought he knew well enough to call friend. Then he glanced at the other men who had also returned in a state of fear one might better associate with old women and young girls. He shifted his gaze back to Sanchez and said, "You are a fool, Sanchez, and your men are the same. You disgust me and I will not forget this."

He turned away, musing on the matter, then clapped his hands and another officer came close, awaiting orders. "You will take more men and you will see that General Santa Anna's orders are carried out. Do you understand?" As he said the other general's name, he stared hard at Sanchez, who looked down at his boots, his ears reddening.

"Yes, sir, consider it done."

"And take Sanchez and his men with you, so that they may see what a successful task looks like when carried out."

But Sanchez and his men refused to return, even when threatened with grave punishment. This told Andrade something that he did not like to think about—that there might be some weak truth in what Sanchez had told him.

"Very well," said the general, rubbing his head. "Others will burn the damned Alamo to the ground. Begin with the barracks."

But when the new patrol approached, they were stopped by the magnificent, freakish sight of a tall, wavering form of a man, a Texan, rising as if by magic from the roof of the very building they hoped to set ablaze. His impossibly long arms were outstretched above his head, held wide apart, and balls of fire danced and leaped and roared in his hands.

The Mexican soldiers screamed; a few turned and fled crying like babies, into the night. But most of them dropped to their knees, covered their eyes with their hands, and screamed in hysterics, begging forgiveness. And still the spirit glared down upon them from on high, his hands holding the dancing balls of flame, his menacing eyes reflecting the same. He did not need to speak; the anger and disgust writ large on his face told them all what he thought of them and their unforgivable task.

Soon they fled, squealing in terror lest the angry spirit hurl the flaming fireballs at them or strike them dead with its devilish, glinting eyes.

Since the turn of the twentieth century, the Alamo has been recognized as one of the most documented haunted spots in the United States. Thousands of people have experienced bizarre, inexplicable occurrences—sights, sounds, smells, feelings, and more—in and around the Alamo, including full apparitions, floating orbs of white light, moans and screams, and the haunting lilt of a lone trumpet playing "El Deguello," or "No Quarter," General Santa Anna's response to the Texans' defiant stance that winter in 1836.

The foreboding tune was played just before the general's final, brutal attack on March 6 that would kill 182 defenders of Texas (including Jim Bowie, Davy Crockett, and William Travis) and leave 1,600 Mexican soldiers dead. It would also leave the Alamo a bombed, smoking ruin, and hundreds of orphans and widows on both sides of the border.

The fight would grow in the public's consciousness as an ultimate act of defiance, of a small force (the Alamo's defenders numbered roughly 189) standing proud against an army (4,000 Mexican soldiers had amassed and attacked the Alamo). It is also remembered as one of the bloodiest battles in the history of America. An aide of General Santa Anna is quoted as saying, "One more such glorious victory and we are finished."

For a decade following the battle, few people ventured near the neglected wreck of the Alamo. Certainly no Mexican soldier dared venture anywhere near it. The fear of ghostly retribution was too ingrained in them, for the soldiers who had been there had talked openly about their horrific experience.

By 1846, along with Texas's admittance to the United States the previous year, the US Army reclaimed the abandoned ruin and, after extensive repairs and reconstruction efforts, the Alamo was once again in use. But it had hardly been unlived in during the previous ten years, as those charged with the task of fixing it and using it would discover. All manner of ghostly inhabitants had settled in.

By the end of the nineteenth century, the city of San Antonio used the buildings for its police headquarters and as a jail. This did not sit well with the spirits of the Alamo's proud defenders, who had no desire to share their eternal home with miscreants, scofflaws, and worse. They let the prisoners, police, and staff know this in no uncertain terms, treating them to all manner of foul behavior: kicks, punches, gougings, shouts, screams, rattling cell bars, moans, cold drafts, and more. Prisoners and their nighttime guards complained so adamantly that they were moved to a different facility.

In death, the ghosts of Alamo defenders, forever dressed in their tattered, bloodied garb, are not allowed to leave their posts, and they spend eternity patrolling the ramparts of the Alamo. But it would seem they are surrounded by enough similar entities to keep them company for a long time to come. The Alamo is stomping ground to a number of ghosts, including a cowboy dressed all in black and soaked to the skin as if from rain. He is believed to be one of twenty-two men sent by William Travis to ride for help—men who never made it back to the fight.

Another ghost pokes his head and shoulders out the window immediately above the church's double doors as if he is looking for the enemy, before ducking back out of sight. Each year in early February, numerous sightings are made of a young, blond-haired boy wandering the historic grounds searching for his father.

Many have reported seeing the ghost of a woman drawing water at the well close by the church, and several staff members, after feeling as though they are being followed, turn to find that a large, glaring Indian had crept up on them. When discovered, he soon vanishes through a wall. Still others claim to have seen the very ghost of Davy Crockett, armed with his flintlock rifle, scouting the surrounding landscape from on high.

Numerous other spirits, as well as shadows and unexplained streaks of light, are seen, all manner of mournful sounds are heard, cold spots and feelings of dread are felt, and the acrid stink of burning wood and gunpowder is smelled by visitors and staff at the Alamo—frequently. In addition to being one of the most haunted spots in the United States, this makes the Alamo the epitome of living history, in a manner of speaking.

Chapter 21

Haunted
Warbonnet Creek

Warbonnet Battlefield Monument
Sioux County, Northwestern Nebraska

Excited and emboldened by the overwhelming success of the Sioux-led victory over Custer's Seventh Cavalry at the Little Big-horn (called Battle of the Greasy Grass by Indians), many bands of Indians, among them the Cheyenne, left reservations in a show of hopeful force. One Cheyenne war party rode into a US Army trap along Hat Creek (now Warbonnet Creek) and though the skirmish was small and short-lived, many people since have experienced the undeniable presence of warriors who have never left the place, feverishly planning a fresh attack that will never come.

Edward Dibney-Stokes stood by the demure stone monument, arms folded against the brief summer chill that goose-bumped his skin. So this was the historic site where William F. "Buffalo Bill" Cody was said to have killed and scalped a Cheyenne warrior chief back on July 17, 1876. Despite the gloomy reminder of what had happened there, he thought it was a pretty spot: waving grasses, blue skies, rolling landscape. He closed his eyes and breathed in the clear, fresh air. Mid-July and he was headed west to start life all over again. He had to smile a little.

He'd been offered a job teaching US history at a boys' school in Montana. He looked forward to the change. And he'd given himself plenty of time to travel west from Boston, so that he might visit various historical sites along the way.

History had always been his passion and now here he was, at another historic monument, a place made famous not for numerous killings, but for one. It could be said, he thought, that it was one man's undoing and another man's making that July day a century before when Buffalo Bill Cody killed and scalped Cheyenne warrior Yellow Hair.

No other death occurred on that battleground on that day. Nonetheless, the site still felt alive with presence; he wasn't sure quite how to describe it, but he didn't feel alone. Neither did he feel comfortable with whoever, whatever, was there with him. He hugged his folded arms tighter, wishing he'd brought his jacket from the car.

"Might as well explore a bit, stretch my legs," he said aloud. He walked down the hill from the monument and stopped. Below him, along the river, the tall grasses were rustling, moving as if something were coursing through them, headed along the creek. Muskrats? He thought little of it, as he was a country boy, having grown up in the sticks in Massachusetts. But he soon stopped still again.

This time not only did he see the grasses continue to move, to part as though someone were crouched down among them, but he swore he heard whispers, many voices, speaking low and in a tongue he was unfamiliar with, but he knew it wasn't English.

His heart fluttered faster; his mouth felt dry. He crouched down for long minutes. And yet all around him he heard voices in that strange language, whispered, hissing, almost as if they were echoing, too many voices at once. He looked back toward the monument and saw a green mist curling upward near it. What could cause that?

As the mist rose, more foggy than smokelike, Edward felt an emotional weight as if the regret and grief of the past few difficult months were all lowering on him, weighing him down, making his heart ache for things he knew he couldn't control. What was it about this place that made him feel this way so suddenly?

He slowly made his way back to his car and drove west as fast as he dared. With each stop his vigor and hopefulness regained the upper emotional hand, but it would be many miles out of northwest Nebraska and into South Dakota before Edward Dibney-Stokes could look back upon his stop at Warbonnet Battlefield Monument with detached curiosity.

And it would be months before he would mention it to one of his new fellow history teachers. The man had opened the conversation by stating that several years before, while vacationing with his wife and two young sons, he had encountered what he believed was his only experience to date with ghosts. He then proceeded to tell Edward what had happened to them when they stopped at the Warbonnet Battlefield Monument. Rushing footsteps, whispering voices speaking in a Native American tongue, hoofbeats, and worst of all, a sense of foreboding that seemed to affect even his two young, normally boisterous sons.

Edward was both relieved and stunned to hear of his new colleague's experience, sounding so similar to his own. And then he related his own tale for the first time.

"Edward," said his friend, nodding, "you know what that language was that you heard, don't you?"

"No, but I have a feeling you're about to tell me." He smiled and sipped his coffee.

"Cheyenne." His friend nodded, no smile on his face. "And they've been recorded and the tapes inspected by experts. It's definitely Cheyenne."

"What is Parkinson doing over there?" The colonel squinted over his shoulder at a corporal who'd dismounted and was bent over, retching into the sage.

"Had too much of that raw water, sir. Been runnin' through the men like . . . well, you know."

"Yes, yes. Well, see to it that the men do little more than wet their lips with the stuff. I'm sure we'll come on cleaner water soon. For now I'm afraid that muddy gargle is all we have. Get him on his horse and let's get moving."

Colonel Wesley Merritt, commanding officer of the US Fifth Cavalry Regiment, sighed and urged his tired mount forward. It was his duty to show fortitude and strength so that his men would keep moving. The last thing he needed was for them to see that whelp hacking his meager breakfast into the weeds.

The sunlight felt as though it were burning holes in his head. *Here it is, early July 1876, and we're supposed to be out here chasing rogue Indians looking to join up with Sitting Bull,* Merritt thought. *Except we haven't seen a single squaw, let alone a plain filled with kill-crazy warriors.* And now he and his men were trudging around this alkali-addled place, looking for Indians who didn't appear to be anywhere near here.

A sudden shout brought his head up, eyes focusing on the plain ahead.

"Rider comin' in! It's the courier, sir."

If there ever was a rider unafraid of being detected, thought Merritt, *it's that red-shirted devil.* He watched as the army courier, William F. Cody, galloped up to the now-halted Fifth Cavalry.

Behind him Merritt heard voices passing among his men as Cody rode up. "It's Buffalo Bill!"

"Colonel," said Cody, reining over to Merritt. He flashed his eyes toward the closer of Merritt's men and spoke in a low voice. "Sir, I have news that I am not at all sure the men should hear from me. I'd rather let you decide that."

"Very well, Cody. Over here." He motioned with his head to his left and they both guided their mounts away from the group.

"Sir, I come bearing bad news—the worst possible, in fact."

Merritt narrowed his eyes and stared at the thirty-year-old Cody. "Out with it, man."

"A few weeks ago a couple hundred men of Custer's Seventh Cavalry were killed, wiped out by Sitting Bull and his bands at Little Bighorn."

"What are you saying? Are you certain?"

"I wish to God that I was wrong. But I am not. It was a massacre. Thousands of Indians met Custer's few hundred."

"And Custer?"

"Why, he's dead, sir. They all are."

"Cody, you must be mistaken." Merritt was even tempted to smile at the absurdity of the very notion. And yet he saw that Cody, normally unflappable, was visibly shaken.

Over the next few minutes, as the news sunk in, Merritt asked all manner of questions of Cody and his worst fears were confirmed. Custer's Seventh Cavalry was part of the three primary columns tasked with converging on the Sioux, and now they were gone.

"That many Indians, Cody?"

"Yes, sir."

That night, as the men set up camp, Colonel Merritt motioned for Cody to join him for a chat.

"Bill, earlier today I received word that more Cheyenne are headed north, probably to Montana to join up with the Sioux."

Cody scratched his beard. "How many of them are there?"

"Best guess is wide—two hundred to three hundred, but that includes full families. It's Morning Star's band."

"Old Dull Knife? So they left the Spotted Tail and Red Cloud bands. Government can't be too happy about that."

"It wasn't unexpected," said Merritt. "But I believe we can intercept them before they even know what's got them riled up."

"And still make it to Montana to help Crook?"

Merritt nodded. "Have to—those are the orders."

"All right then. What can I do?"

Merritt smiled. "Glad you offered, because I have a plan." The two men lit cigars and spoke for the better part of an hour.

Days later the wagons of the US Fifth Cavalry had with them rumbled to a stop alongside Warbonnet Creek. But other than the drivers, there were few men in sight. Those who were visible only made the convoy seem to be a poorly armed transport train headed north. They stayed this way, hunkered down alongside the creek, for a few hours.

Merritt had told the men that they would be in danger, but not as much as the Cheyenne. But to keep their ears and eyes alert. It didn't take long before, true to Merritt's word, ululating shouts echoed across the breezy vale and the scant party of cavalrymen looked up from their make-work tasks to see six mounted Cheyenne warriors thundering down at them.

The soldiers weren't worried, though. The wagons were loaded with armed soldiers and the surrounding landscape bristled with sharpshooters, all waiting for a crack at the main body of Cheyenne, of which these six were but a scouting war party.

Within seconds a force of mounted cavalrymen broke from cover. Astride a strong mount, Buffalo Bill Cody soon outdistanced his fellow charging soldiers. He found himself vaulting a short rise and coming up close to a lone chiefly warrior adorned with a magnificent feathered headdress. The two foes eyed one another but a moment, the thunder of hooves approaching behind each, the shouts and cries of battle lust ringing in the air, and that was enough to spur the two men into action. They drew on each other.

Cody's Winchester fired, found its mark, and dropped Yellow Hair's horse. The Indian tumbled to the ground, then gained his feet as Cody's horse lost its footing and stumbled. Cody rolled with it and came up with his Winchester in time to see Yellow Hair taking aim with a Colt revolver. Before the Indian could fire, Cody cranked two rounds into the warrior, dropping him in his tracks.

Soldiers were scattered all about him now, firing and chasing down other Indians. Cody slipped out his sheath knife and yanked Yellow Hair's head back. With a few quick strokes of the sharp blade, he lifted the Indian's scalp free. Buffalo Bill Cody held the bloody souvenir aloft, shouting, "First scalp for Custer!"

The Cheyenne broke like wind-scattered leaves and though the Fifth Cavalry gave hard chase, no side lost any other lives . . . that day. Sadly, many other lives would soon be lost, most of them Native American. Though the battle took place at Hat Creek, the location is now known as Warbonnet Creek. Though brief, the confrontation signaled the US Army's eventual dominance in what came to be known as the Great Sioux War of 1876–77.

Cody's battle has lasted long in history and did as much as any other episode to build the career of William F. "Buffalo Bill" Cody. In the ensuing years, his man-to-man fight with Yellow Hair (often mistakenly referred to as "Yellow Hand") was stretched into fable and made legendary in print, on stage, and in Cody's own touring show, known as "Buffalo Bill's Wild West." During the show he reenacted the brief skirmish and displayed Yellow Hair's scalp, war bonnet, and other accoutrements.

Despite his anger at the death of Custer and of the soldiers at the Little Bighorn, Cody was a lifelong advocate of and friend to American Indians, and is famously quoted as saying, "Every Indian outbreak that I have ever known has resulted from broken promises and broken treaties by the government."

Perhaps the unseen warriors experienced so often at the site of the Warbonnet Creek Battlefield—the ones who creep through the swaying grasses and whisper to their fellow warriors, who delight in the thrill of the hunt—are the spirits of Indians who fought for the freedom of their unfettered lives before the white men's incursions into their homeland.

Part Five

RANCH, MANSION & MARKET

Chapter 22

Ghostly Guilt of the Winchester Heir

Winchester Mystery House
San Jose, California

Following his death in 1881, the heir to the fortune of the famed "gun that won the West," William Wirt Winchester, told his wife via a séance that she must build a house to accommodate the spirits of all the people killed by his family's invention. Sarah Winchester spent the next thirty-eight years overseeing round-the-clock construction on her ever-expanding home, spending $5.5 million on a sprawling mansion that included 160 rooms, 950 doors, and 10,000 windows. At the Winchester Mystery House, now a museum, visitors have experienced roving balls of light, apparitions floating through walls, organ music, whisperings, and banging and slamming. Few visitors leave disappointed . . . or unafraid.

The rumbling woke Sarah Winchester. This night she'd chosen the Daisy Room, as she had many other nights in the past, though never for more than one night at a time. She liked to keep a few steps ahead of the bad spirits, literally, by leaving the séance room each night, traveling throughout the massive house seemingly at random, turning on a dime, then disappearing into what appeared to be a broom closet—but actually led to a hidden narrow staircase, or into an entire hidden wing. She took great pains when planning the construction of her house to be sure it was filled with such odd doors and hidden passages.

In this way, night after night, she repeated the cat-and-mouse games, moving with plan and cunning to keep just ahead of the "bad" spirits that constantly sought to haunt her and disrupt her all-consuming work. And this night had been no exception. She thought she had successfully evaded the malevolents, but the rumbling, the crashing—something was different, wrong somehow. Even before bed, Sarah Winchester had sensed an almost palpable feeling of dread in the very air. And so, she had gone to bed more troubled than usual.

Had she done all she could to appease them? Or were the spirits finally turning against her, even after the lavish dinners in the dining room, complete with solid-gold place settings, the finest wines, and imported delicacies. All for the spirits, all offered in her never-ending quest to keep the victims of Winchester weapons appeased.

Or were the evil spirits finally catching up with her? The ones who found their way into her home, the ones who sought to undermine her life's work, the ones whose sole mission it was, as each day's light wore down and the shadows lengthened, to find her and . . . No! It was too much to bear thinking about. The evil spirits would not win, could not win. She simply would not let them.

After all, she had been instructed by her dear departed husband, William, with the help of a spiritualist, to purchase a home in which all the spirits of all the people ever killed by a Winchester rifle might find solace. Above all, he had said, it must be under constant, round-the-clock construction, twenty-four hours a day, each day of the week, year in and year out. This she had done since 1884, and she fully expected to continue to do so until death took her to meet her dear sweet baby, Annie, and her William. It was blood that the guns had drawn, William had relayed, and it would be blood money that would appease them—but only if she followed his instructions.

Sarah Winchester lay in the dark, feeling the house rumble and shake, hearing the sounds of glass shattering in other rooms, wood ripping and splintering, bookcases crashing to the floor. And she knew that somehow she had failed her dead husband, failed in her life's mission.

The entire front section of the grand home, a massive forward wing that contained numerous rooms and a tower, began to rumble and shake, then entire walls collapsed. Her screams went unheard. Soon, though, many of her would-be rescuers, men who were in her employ, rushed to the main house, saw the collapsed section, and began pawing the wreckage, unsure just where Mrs. Winchester had bedded down for that night. Had she been in that front wing? No one knew for some time, until a chambermaid confirmed their fears. It would be hours before they could get to her, all convinced she had perished in the collapse. But she hadn't.

Long after the worst of it, as she lay in the dark, trapped in the wreckage of the Daisy Room, Sarah Winchester had ample time to speculate about what had happened to her beloved home. Appease the good spirits and outwit the bad, that was her mission. Somehow the spirits had been offended.

In the coming weeks, she had the debris cleared away. Then she sealed off the damaged front section of the house—forever. Despite the fact that a massive earthquake had rocked nearby San Francisco, she felt certain that the damage to her beloved home had been caused by displeased spirits. She vowed to redouble her efforts, and soon had her builders add on to the house in a different direction, continuing with renewed vigor their around-the-clock pace.

Tish Pemberly groaned and hugged herself tighter as she tagged along at the rear of the group. The sooner this tour was over, the better. All she wanted to do was get back out in the California sunshine. She'd been eager enough to visit her grandparents, anything to get off the farm in Iowa, she was so bored there. But visiting her grandparents hadn't been all she had expected. They'd insisted on taking her to an amusement park, and out to eat—good Lord, she was going to gain weight and never look good in her new bikini—when all she wanted to do was lie on the beach and soak up the California sun. When was she going to get the chance to do that again? Not in Iowa, that's for sure. Once again she found herself tagging along behind the old folks, touring some dark old mansion that made no sense. Some place called the Winchester Mystery House.

It was not so much mysterious as crazy, thought Tish. Hallways that ended with a door that, if you stepped through, you'd fall two floors and break your legs—or worse. And then there were the staircases that went to nowhere at all. What sort of a nut job would build such a place? She knew the tour guides were probably as bored as she was, leading people through the same rooms day after day. Thank God they didn't have to see every single one of the 160 rooms the tour people said were in the house. Tish knew that if it were up to her grandpa, they would look into each and every one.

She looked up from half-admiring a crystal-fringed lamp sitting on a side table. All this money, she thought, wasted on spirits and ghosts and ghouls. The old Winchester lady had to have been certifiably crazy. Who else would spend millions on a house, 95 percent of which would never see use? She looked up and noticed that the tour group had moved on. She thought she could hear voices murmuring, and headed toward the quickly receding sounds. "Hey, anybody there?"

Soon she heard nothing, and wondered which of the three doors she should leave by, and where to go after that. Tish cursed herself for not remembering the route out of here. As she looked around the richly appointed sitting room, she saw a colorful stained-glass window and headed toward it. Maybe she could orient herself if she could see outside. As she squinted through a clear prism-like pane of the wavy, multicolored leaded glass, she saw nothing but a jumble of rooflines, chimneys, and windowed peaks, all part of the same house.

A rustling sound drew her from the window, and when she turned she saw a small, old, gray-haired woman in a black dress standing across the room, the diffuse colors from another stained-glass window lighting her from behind. The woman's face was rounded, her arms hanging at her sides. The dress looked like dull black satin, lots of folds and flouncy-looking layers of an out-of-date fashion, definitely not something Tish would ever be caught wearing in public, or at home.

The old woman stared at her, her head slightly lowered as if she were sizing up Tish, regarding her from head to toe. But her little dark eyes never left Tish's. It was kind of freaky.

"Are you one of the tour guides? I . . . I like your cos-tume. It's pretty." *It's not at all,* she thought to herself. *It looks old and uncomfortable, just like her. And if this person is a tour guide, someone was snoozing at the switch when they hired her. She has all the friendliness of a stick.*

Tish sighed and leaned against the wall, her purse clunking against a small chair, nudging it from its place. The other woman's eyes went wide and Tish swore she heard an animal-like growling sound come from the old lady's throat.

"Chill, will you? The tour group left me behind. Look, I'm just trying to find a way out of this place. I mean, come on, who in their right mind would build such a firetrap?" Tish decided she'd give anything to be on the beach right now. Heck, she'd give anything to be back with the tour group.

She had been staring right at the old woman, couldn't help it, in fact. Her dark eyes seemed to pin her somehow. She didn't see her draw closer, closer. . . . And once the old woman moved away from the window that had backlit her, Tish's face blanched, drained of any sun-baked hue she had managed to gain. Her eyes widened, her mouth sagged. . . . The old woman wasn't touching the floor, not her dress, no shoes were visible, and she moved as if she were propelled on an unseen breeze, like a puck on an air-hockey table.

Was this another of the tricks the place played on visi-tors? They'd said the place was haunted, as had her grand-parents on the ride over. But at the time that had seemed foolish, just another come-on to get her to go with them.

The old woman floated closer, closer . . . close enough that Tish could see her face, the angry eyes dark like black glass. As she drew closer, Tish felt a wash of frigid air, like one of those strange patches of cold in Driscoll's pond when she went swimming with her friends back home. But this cold was coming from the old woman, as if she were generating it, like a block of floating ice. But it was what Tish didn't see that dragged the scream from her trembling mouth.

She could see *through* the old, gray-haired woman's skin, could see the room through her as if her skin were a gauzy curtain. The closer she drew, the easier it was to see through her, even the dress, which before had appeared black and solid as heavy drapes.

Tish screamed and covered her eyes with her trembling hands.

"There you are! What's the matter, dear? Tish? Tish?"

The girl cracked open her eyes and saw a woman's arms reach for her, grab her shoulders. She tensed, backed up, tried to squirm away. "No! Get away! Get away, you awful thing!"

She struck out, then hands grabbed her wrists and a man's voice shouted, "Tish! Get a hold of yourself!"

And she looked into her grandfather's face, her grandmother standing beside him, and beyond, in the room, the rest of the tour group. She broke down, sobbing, and wrapped her arms around her grandfather. She'd never been so glad to see someone she knew. As she hugged him, she scanned the rest of the room—six other people including the tour guide, all looking at her as if she'd lost her marbles. But there was no sign of an old woman with gray hair and wearing a black dress.

It took a few minutes more before she could tell them all what had happened to her. And the tour guide, though interested, didn't seem surprised. But she did verify that Tish was not crazy. She had merely met the ghost of Mrs. Sarah Winchester. And evidently Mrs. Winchester wasn't fond of what Tish had to say about the home, her very life's labor. A place she still roamed and protected, even in death.

For the first time in a long time, Tish wished she was back home in Iowa.

In 1884 Sarah Winchester had traveled to California with the express purpose of purchasing a decent-sized home in the midst of significant acreage. The property had to be large enough to accommodate her plans for constant expansion to accommodate the innumerable "good" spirits of those killed by her husband's family's invention. She eagerly anticipated what would become her life's mission.

Since losing her first and only child, Annie, dead in 1866 at six weeks of age of a wasting disease, and then her William, dead in 1881 of tuberculosis, she had been inconsolable. Glad of the permanent distraction her dead husband's séance-fueled instructions provided, Sarah Winchester embarked on a lifelong quest the likes of which the world has rarely seen.

Employing scores of carpenters to work around the clock, seven days a week, 365 days a year, year in, year out, sawing, hammering, planning, painting, filling, roofing, removing, refurbishing, and generally remodeling the Winchester mansion. Even the Great Earthquake of 1906 barely slowed progress on the sprawling pile. After the temblor, she had the house's damaged front section closed off, not daring to risk offending any spirits that might still find it homey. No one would enter those rooms again until well after the old woman's death in 1922.

The massive, sprawling house was surrounded by grounds that were just as impressive and included gardens, a commercial fruit orchard, and housing for her numerous employees and their families. According to many firsthand accounts, Mrs. Sarah Winchester was a stern but kind employer, and a sane and savvy businesswoman who also happened to have a powerful belief in the afterlife.

Mrs. Winchester spent $5.5 million of her $20 million fortune outfitting her ever-expanding home with the finest crystal, gold, and silver chandeliers and Tiffany art glass, imported artwork, wallpapers, lighting fixtures, bathtubs from Switzerland, and other impressive architectural elements from around the world. Her copious purchases were stored in the house itself, in anticipation of their eventual installation. But when she died in 1922, the house still contained numerous rooms brimming with the lavish imported accoutrements.

Now a popular tourist hot spot, the world-famous Winchester Mystery House also contains Mrs. Sarah Winchester, or rather her spirit, as numerous visitors, workers, psychics, and tour guides will attest. But her restless shade is not alone. Other Winchester House specters include the apparition of a laboring man dressed in overalls and pushing a wheelbarrow, most notably in the basement.

Visitors and tour guides also continue to feel cold spots, the light strokes of unseen hands on their arms, cheeks, and hair. Likewise, roving balls of light and the sounds of breathing and footsteps still echo throughout the many empty rooms of the Winchester Mystery House, an abode fit for an army of ghosts—with rooms to spare.

Chapter 23

Prairie Parties
at 101 Ranch

The Miller Brothers' 101 Ranch
Kay County, Oklahoma

In 1879 Colonel George W. Miller established the 101 Ranch on 110,000 acres in Kay County, Oklahoma. The 101 had its own school, stores, cafe, hotel, meat-packing plant, dairy, magazine, newspaper, three thousand inhabitants, and a world-famous touring Wild West show. Eventually the buildings were torn down and the land was sold. Soon after, as locals passed by what remained of the ranch—foundations and old roads—they heard laughter, singing, and bands playing. Today people travel from near and far to hear the phantom hootenannies of the famed 101 Ranch. A few have even dared to venture into the cellars of the old mansion. . . .

The concrete-walled basement was the only thing left of what had once been one of the grandest homes in all of Oklahoma. But tonight it was just a quiet hole as black as ink, just like Bean hoped it would be. Bean didn't buy into that hokum about ghosts and ghouls prancing about the place, but he knew that all girls did—and especially his girl, Dory—and what's more, he suspected that his best friend, Jason, believed in spooks, too.

So Bean had come up with that excuse to go back to the truck for more beer. He'd parked it in the lane leading up to the foundation of the old 101 Ranch's White House, and he hoped it was just out of view of where they were perched near the Miller family burial plot.

This was all Jason's idea, anyway. He'd insisted they bring the girls out here, ever since his Uncle Rupe had told him he'd been out here not long ago, late afternoon into dusk, and had heard Indian powwow drums and singing and laughing. Just like a phantom cowboy party, the old man had said, only there weren't any people around. He also swore he'd seen "shades," he called them, darting between those old concrete silos that were still standing. Caught a glimpse of them just out of the corner of his eye, looked like people's shadows darting here and there. Said it was some sort of leftover energy from the people who used to live at the ranch.

Bean chuckled to himself. Jason's Uncle Rupe had probably had a snort or three of something, then had commenced to seeing and hearing all sorts of things. Bean checked his pocket for his flashlight but didn't turn it on. They'd be coming to look for him soon. He'd moan and carry on—oh, he vowed to make this a night to remember! He was planning on spooking the others so hard they'd never, ever forget it.

And Bean was still waiting in the dank dark ten minutes later. How long would it take them to miss him? He was beginning to get a little peeved—he truly had not expected them to take so long to look for him. Then he heard a far-off voice, could have been Jason's, but it was still too distant-sounding to make out what it was saying. He folded his arms across his chest and waited some more.

Despite the fact that it was a hot summer night and he was in jeans and his best shirt, the snap-front, blue-check one, it was oddly cold down in the basement. Must be the dirt floor and cement walls. Probably some snakes or rats down here, too, dang it. And then there was that voice again, but closer now. Only he wasn't sure it was from the direction he'd left the others. Or maybe it was; hard to tell what direction was what once he'd gotten down in here.

A quick sound, like a dog's claws scratching stone, sounded low and off to his right. He stood still, narrowed his eyes. What was that? Probably a damn rat. Good thing he wasn't on the ground, rolling around with Dory. He smiled at the thought. Time enough for that later. If she forgave him for giving her the fright of her life, that is. He almost giggled.

To his right, hot breath pushed into his face, and from the left, a whispered male voice said, "That's right, that's right. Okay, then. . . ." Bean's throat clamped shut and he lashed out with his left arm. It swung wide and his knuckles rapped against the concrete wall he'd been leaning against. The pain snapped him from his moment of fright. "Who in the heck . . . ?"

Bean thrust his other hand into his jeans pocket even as his left smarted and throbbed where it had hit the concrete. His fingers curled around the flashlight and he drew it out with a shaking hand. He forced the button with his thumb—nothing. No light. He felt a shout or worse building up in him. *God, no, don't let me scream,* he thought. *Anything but that. What if Jason and the girls hear me?* And then whispers and footsteps drew even closer.

"Jason, is that you? Enough of this business, now. Ain't no need to go on and on to rile me. I ain't scared. . . . Jason? I've about had enough." The boots-on-gravel sounds drew closer, he felt hot breath on his cheek again, then something brushed by him, just touching his pants legs. Bean bolted to his right, hoping he could find his way out of the cellar hole. He'd also begun shouting at the top of his voice. He didn't care anymore who or what it was—even if it was Jason, he'd had enough. Let them laugh at him, laugh all they wanted. He had to get out of this hole in the ground.

Bean rapped the flashlight against the heel of his hand but it wouldn't even flicker. God, but he should have just gotten the beer from the truck like he said he was going to.

Tired of waiting by an old concrete silo, Jason and the two girls decided to pack it in and go looking for Bean, who they were sure would try to spook them. Then Liz shushed them and put a hand on Jason's forearm. He liked the warm feeling it gave him. Then he heard it, too—someone singing in harmony. Or rather a whole lot of someones. And not too far off. He couldn't make out the tune, but it sounded old-timey and happy, and mingling with it were the sounds of laughing voices and occasional yips and yeehaws!

Though the sounds were pleasant, Jason and the girls held their breath and the hair on their necks stood up. Could they be the sounds Uncle Rupe had told him about?

"What is that, Jason?"

Before he could answer, they heard footsteps, perhaps a few dozen yards behind them, then a voice said, "Nah, nah, won't do, won't do at all. . . ."

Jason stood, put his hands out as if to corral the girls behind him, but they all pushed close together. "Who . . . who's there?" Jason fumbled for his flashlight, flicked it on, but there was no one in sight, nothing but grass and the few remains of the buildings that once occupied the place. Meanwhile, the singing continued, and mingling with it, they heard a distant, steady *thud thud thud,* like tribal drums. It sounded as if a whole party was taking place somewhere just out of sight, the sounds of it carrying to them on a light Oklahoma summer night's breeze.

Calm down, old boy, Bean told himself, aware now that his own breathing wasn't the only breathing he heard. There was another one, close by in the dark. He rapped the flashlight again and it flicked on. He held his breath as he spun the beam toward the other breathing sound, but there was nothing but blackness and the crumbly concrete wall beyond.

Something touched his hair! Bean screamed and spun, flailing. But again, there was nothing there. It had felt for all the world like when Dory ran her hand down the back of his head, caressing him. But Dory wasn't down there, was she?

Desperate now to find the way out, he worked the flashlight's weak beam over the walls, found the black space where the steps led up and out, and bolted for them. As he gained the top step he felt a rush of hot air, like breath, on the back of his neck. He shrieked again and kicked up gravel as he headed toward his pickup. And he swore he heard a low, throaty chuckle stop just behind him on the cellar steps.

"Bean! There you are, man. We been looking all over for you." Jason's flashlight beam rested on Bean's face. "Hey, you all right? You're breathing hard. You look like you seen a—"

Bean's index finger came up and he pointed it straight at his friend's face. "Don't you say it. Just don't you say it! Now, everybody, let's get on out of here. Meet you at the diner in town." *The one with all the lights and people,* he thought to himself.

Jason angled his truck out first, so Bean fell in behind, Dory quiet on the seat beside him. Normally he didn't mind her chatter, but he was glad that tonight she was silent. He figured he might tell them all once they got to the diner. Or not.

As he steered his pickup truck out of the lane, trying like heck to not roostertail the gravel behind him, Bean glanced in the rearview mirror and saw two points of yellow glowing light just about where the cellar hole of the White House sat in the dark. They grew smaller as he drove away, trying to swallow back his fear and choke off the scream welling in his throat. For he was certain those eyes were staring straight at him. He still felt that hot breath on his neck, and he bet if he listened real close, he could hear that throaty laughing sound, too.

In 1879 Colonel George W. Miller established the 101 Ranch in Kay County, Oklahoma. By the time he died in 1903, he had made it into one of the largest working ranches in the country. After the Colonel's death, his three sons assumed management of the entire sprawling operation.

Two years later, under their supervision, they began a new venture and created one of the most famous of all the touring Wild West shows of the day. The 101 Ranch Wild West Show rivaled Buffalo Bill Cody's for sheer extravagance, and for two decades it toured the United States, South America, and Europe, dazzling packed crowds with the skills of the finest and most talented Western performers of the day, including Will Rogers, Pawnee Bill, Bulldoggin' Bill Pickett, ropers, riders, and more.

When this massive touring outfit wasn't on the road, the Miller Ranch was the nexus of operations—and fun—for the scores of folks involved in the business. Summer nights would see them all gathered around campfires, singing and whooping it up until the wee hours. But eventually, as with all good things, this, too, came to an end.

By 1927 the oldest of the brothers, Joe, was killed by carbon monoxide poisoning. The middle brother, Zack, died in 1929 in a car accident, and the youngest of the brothers, George, did his best to run the once-burgeoning empire, even in the midst of his grief. And he wasn't able to do it.

Due largely to the Great Depression, the Miller family's substantial holdings were ravaged. A town's worth of buildings were torn down, and the massive ranch's lands were sold off bit by bit, until by 1931 barely one acre existed around the three-story White House, and then that, too, was sold off and leveled. Two decades later, in 1952, George, the last of the Miller boys, died at his home in Texas.

In the years to follow, scores of tourists, locals, and travelers all reported hearing the distinct sounds of phantom parties, the strains of lilting cowboy tunes, yodels, and whooping and sing-alongs, the unmistakable noises of the 101's famed hootenannies from days gone by all carried on the wind. But when they explored, they could find no one around, merely the remnants of the once-great 101 Ranch, the stone foundation of the famed old White House, a few lone silos and smaller buildings, but no one in them. At least no one alive.

Today some folks who visit the site still experience more than they bargain for. They don't just hear the sounds of laughter and gaiety. They see shapes fleeting zephyr-like from place to place, out from behind the silos, darting for cover behind nearby sheds. Overly curious tourists have reported hearing flurries of whispered voices close to their ears as they venture into the dark basement rooms of the foundations of the White House. Still others report being pinched, their hair stroked from behind. They turn and find . . . no one.

But none of these occurrences stop local youths from doing their best to match the eerie wind-borne sounds of century-old ghostly revelers. Though sometimes it doesn't turn out quite the way they had planned it.

Chapter 24
Pike Place Ghosts

Pike Place Market
Seattle, Washington

Called America's most famous farmers' market, Pike Place Market is also known as the most haunted location in the Northwest. The market brims with all manner of paranormal activity, some of which predates the market's 1907 opening, and includes regular sightings of the ghostly daughter of Chief Seattle, sometimes seen with an Indian boy. It is probable that many of the market's other numerous ghosts, known as the "Shadow People," were once clients at the city's first mortuary, once housed nearby. . . .

The tour of haunted Pike Place Market was to meet at the Gum Wall, something that Gwen wasn't so sure she wanted to stand anywhere near. She read about it, figured she'd end up seeing it and would have to take pictures of it for the story she was working on. But seeing it was something different—a fifty-foot wall covered in chewed gum that people had stuck to the brick up to a height of about fifteen feet.

When she'd bought a sandwich earlier at the deli upstairs, the cashier had proudly declared the Gum Wall as one of the world's top "germiest" attractions. And now that Gwen saw it, she had to agree that it looked pretty funky. But the more she stared at it, the more she realized it was sort of intriguing and not without its charms—if you looked past the fact that at one time all those little blobs of color had been smacking around in people's mouths.

"Are you here for the ghost tour?"

Gwen turned and saw a young couple standing in the shadows, arms around each other, matching scarves. She had to smile. *Ah, young love,* she thought. "Yep, sure am," said Gwen. "Wanted to see what sort of dog-and-pony show they put on for the tourists."

The young man eyed her warily, half-smiling. "What do you mean?"

"I'm sorry, I'm a natural-born skeptic," said Gwen. "And a journalist. The second requires the first, I think. I don't buy into ghost stories, that sort of thing. Why?" She reached into her pocket for her recorder. "Do you two believe in ghosts?"

"Sure," they both said at the same time, then laughed.

The young man said, "In fact, we see them all the time. Princess Angeline's your best bet. We bumped into her not long ago, by the wooden column in the lower level of the market."

"Right," said Gwen, trying not to laugh. They seemed so sincere. "Well, that's handy to know. You'll forgive me if I don't rush down there and take a peek."

"Oh, but it's the best time to see her," said the young woman, "once the market's closed for the day. She's a little shy."

Gwen forced a smile. Was everyone in this city so . . . gullible? Best change the subject, she thought. "I'm writing a piece for a newspaper back east and the editor wants the 'alternative' Seattle, which is a redundancy, from what I've gathered."

"Then you're not from here."

"No, no. Never been before. I always wanted to visit the Pacific Northwest, though. And I must say, it's beautiful. You guys from here?"

"Yeah," said the young man. "We're here for good. We love it."

"We'll never leave." The girl hugged him closer.

Gwen nodded, aware she should be asking them better questions, get some color for the article, but it had been a long day and she was getting cold and tired and cranky. She smiled weakly at them and looked up the street. Where was that tour guide? *I just want to get this thing over with,* she thought. *Get back to my hotel and make it an early night.* She had a lot of places to cover tomorrow.

"So," she said, turning back to the young couple, "what do you guys . . . do?" They were gone. She'd only turned away for two seconds, but they were nowhere to be seen. And there wasn't any place for them to hide or vanish—she should be able to see them hurrying away.

"Are you here for the ghost tour?"

Gwen shrieked and spun back around. A tall young woman in a black wool overcoat and a red beret stood before her, smiling. "I usually get that *after* we're under way."

Other people were walking up behind her.

Gwen reached out, cautiously touching the young woman's sleeve, then squeezed her arm. "You're real, right?"

"So far," she said, smiling. "Why?"

"You . . . wouldn't believe me if I told you."

"Try me."

Josh finished washing the vegetables and started chopping lettuce. He hated being alone in the restaurant this early, but it would be another hour before Louis came in to help him get ready for the breakfast crowd. He had wanted a job like this for years, figured it was the way you learn to become a chef, and he kind of liked it—except for the waking up early part. And the freaky ghost stuff.

The idea of ghosts—heck, everyone knew they were all over the place around Pike Place Market—hadn't bothered him before. But then again, he'd never worked in a haunted place before, at least not that he knew of. He wished Louis hadn't told him that the building used to be a funeral parlor. And that the room where he was slicing oozing tomatoes had been where they embalmed people. The thought of it gave him goose bumps. And now that he was alone in the place every morning, six days a week, weird things had started to happen, and more frequently.

Got to stop thinking about this stuff, thought Josh. He turned to grab another bowl off the counter behind him, and as he turned back, he saw his big chef's knife spinning around like a compass needle. Then it settled, trembling on the counter, the point toward him. Joshua knew he wasn't seeing things. This was the worst weird thing yet to happen to him here. He didn't know what to do; the knife seemed to be quivering right there on the counter, just like in a movie. Like if he made a grab for it, it might shoot straight into his gut.

That's when the cold air passed through him, as if someone had suddenly cranked an air conditioner on high right in front of him, right *in* him. But it was February, and these were ghosts. And as if he were wearing headphones, he heard a knot of high-pitched voices, like kids' voices, in both ears, laughing and wheezing. Then just behind him, he heard lots of fast footsteps, like bare feet slapping on the tiled floor.

He turned his head, but there was no one there, just the big locked door to the basement. The basement, Louis had told him, where years ago when the place was refurbished, they'd found forgotten shelves full of small, numbered urns with ashes inside. The ashes, Louis had said, were of local orphans farmed out as free laborers at Pike Place Market.

They must have liked their work, thought Josh, *because they're still here.* He looked at the knife, still quivering on the counter, still pointing at him, and he bolted for the door; the unmistakable sound of children laughing followed him until he slammed the door and locked it.

Within minutes Josh called Louis and quit. Louis had sighed and seemed to understand. As Josh walked fast down the sidewalk to his car, he wondered whether the food court at the mall outside of town was haunted.

In what has been called the most haunted spot in the entire Northwest, in the entire state of Washington, and certainly in all of Seattle, Pike Place Market is the ideal bridge between the Old West and the new. The location has a rich history that long predates the market. It is believed that part of the market is built on ground sacred to the local Indian tribes who were forced to give up their land to the whites and move to reservations. This may account for the fact that the market is so popular with Native American spirits. It is also possible that a few of these spectral denizens were once clients at the city's first mortuary, also once housed on market premises. It could also be that the remnants of the city's first mortuary nearby have provided an ideal spot for paranormal activity. . . .

The Pike Place Market encompasses nine acres and is visited annually by ten million people, many of them tourists, making it one of Seattle's top attractions. The market offers numerous buildings filled with more than 200 shops, markets, and eateries, plus 190 craftspeople and 100 farmers who rent day-table space. In addition, the complex hosts roughly 250 street performers and buskers, and eight of its buildings are home to 300 apartments, many for low-income elderly.

Per the 1855 Treaty of Point Elliott, the Duwamish Indians were required to give up their land and relocate to reservations. But in disobeying the order, Kikisoblu, or Kick-is-om-lo, in her native language of Lushootseed, eldest daughter of the Duwamish tribe's famous Chief Seattle (for whom the city is named), unwittingly made herself one of the Old West's most valuable ambassadors. Through her presence she provided a valuable link between the many Native American inhabitants of the region with the more recent white settlers. Kikisoblu, or "Princess Angeline" as she came to be called by Seattle's early white residents, lived in a small shack at the foot of Pike Street, overlooking the water. She kept body and soul together by selling handmade baskets on street corners and taking in laundry.

During this period she was photographed numerous times by famous Old West photographer Edward Curtis. She was well regarded by many of Seattle's white founding families, though it is said she threw rocks at children who pestered her. She was a familiar stooped figure often seen slowly walking throughout the waterfront neighborhoods. She died on May 31, 1896, at the approximate age of eighty-five. Princess Angeline's well-attended service was held in a local church and her canoe-shaped coffin was decorated for the occasion. Though she passed away more than a decade before the Pike Place Market opened, she nonetheless haunts the locale, in part because the market encompasses the spot on which she used to live.

But in death as she was in life, Princess Angeline is no spooky specter. As the market's most visible and most famous supernatural resident, she has been seen countless times, usually at the lower level, beside a wooden column that has reportedly exuded waves of cold and emits a strange wavery aura that appears as an anomaly when photographed. Princess Angeline's ghost moves about slowly, as she did when alive, cane in hand, red kerchief on her head and her hunched frame shuffling along. Only now she doesn't touch the ground, and she has been seen to change color—shifting from white to blue and lavender.

Another spirit, known as the "Fat Lady Barber," continues her living habit of singing lullabies. This she did for her unfortunate barber customers in the 1950s, who would doze off in the chair long enough for her to filch cash from their pockets. A rather large woman at roughly three hundred pounds, she died at the market in the early 1970s after falling through a weak floor on her balcony. Her spirit now spends the wee hours singing lullabies, heard by the market's nighttime cleaning crews.

The ghost of a young boy haunts a spot now occupied by a bead store. During recent renovations, a basket of colorful beads was found in a wall space. This technically was not possible since the bead store didn't exist the last time the wall space had been exposed—there was literally no way into the wall space. Paranormal investigators suspect the ghost just wanted to play with the beads. The same ghost is responsible for tampering with the store's cash register and playing with puppets in another shop.

Other ghosts throughout the market have been seen staring out windows, balefully watching shoppers. Arthur Goodwin, nephew of the founder of the market's original developer, had a hand in running the market for more than two decades, from 1918 to 1941, and can still be seen gazing down at the bustling hub from what used to be his office. He has also been seen practicing his golf swing in his old work digs.

Another intriguing Pike Place Market spook is believed to be that of a woman called Madame Nora, who ran a shop called the Temple of Destiny in the market's early days. She was a notorious practitioner of crystal-ball gazing and psychic projection. Her spirit is said to inhabit her old crystal ball and is now in residence in a magic shop, where she is most noted for moving items about the shop in the night.

In one of the market's delis, on the lower level, staff have repeatedly heard angry ghosts shouting and engaged in fisticuffs in a walk-in freezer. Yet when the door is opened, the frigid space is devoid of people.

All these ghosts and more, who most often come out at night and are referred to locally as the "Shadow People," seem to happily inhabit one of the West's most haunted spots, Pike Place Market. But it is Chief Seattle himself, exiled leader of the Duwamish tribe, who spoke words in 1854 that go a long way toward explaining the market's—and the city of Seattle's—preponderance of paranormal episodes.

Indeed, given the content of his long-ago speech, it may well be the first and last word on the subject: "When the memory of my tribe shall become a myth among white men, when your children think themselves alone in the field, the store, the shop—they will not be alone. When you think your streets deserted, they will throng with the returning hosts that once filled and still love this land, for the dead are not powerless."

Part Six

COWBOY, INDIAN & BEAST

Chapter 25

Neches River
Hell Riders

The Neches River
Northwest of San Antonio, Texas

An 1870 cattle drive from Texas to Abilene, Kansas, halted at the Neches River, or Rio Nueces—beyond it sat a sodbuster's ranch house. The trail boss gave the sign and three thousand head of Texas longhorns boiled across the river and trampled everything, including the ranch house, the rancher, his wife, and children. Within five years, each of the eight coldhearted cowboys died. Forever after, on certain summer nights, that stretch of Texas's Neches River becomes an unholy, thundering mass of gleaming-eyed cattle- and cowboy-shaped clouds that shake the earth and sky. Elsewhere in Texas, hellish screams accompany the smokelike ghosts of cattle and cowboys at Stampede Mesa.

"Now look at that, boys! We got ourselves a sodbuster who thinks he's got some sort of rights. Well . . . bull-and-a-half, he does!" The trail boss reined his buckskin hard and faced the seven men gathered behind him. "I don't aim to let a dirt digger and his damn fence force me to go anywhere but where I need to get these cattle. I use the same trail every year, year in and out, to get my cattle to market up in Abilene. When I come through here last year, there weren't nobody here, no fences, no soddy, no corral, no nothing. Now look at it. . . ."

"But boss," said Corcoran, "he's got hisself a wife and children. I seen 'em head on into the house as we rode up."

Just as the boss was about to shout the man down, Smitty, a small, wiry fellow who rode drag, eating dust at the back of the herd, tugged down his grime-caked bandanna and nodded past the boss. "That sodbuster's fixin' to do somethin' dumb, boss."

The big man turned back around in the saddle to see that the farmer had reemerged from the house cradling a shotgun. He strode well beyond his house and looked back at it once, and the door slowly closed from the inside. He walked toward the cluster of men a-horseback, and stopped fifty yards from them, plenty close for them all to hear what he had to shout.

"You no-good cowpunchers best get off my property and stay off! You even think of setting one foot of your scabby, no-account cattle onto my place, there will be hell to pay and I'm the one who's going to dole out a heapin' helpin' to each of you!" He thumbed back the hammers on the double-barrel, then said to the boss, "And the first one to get it will be you, fat boy."

For a few long moments, no one said anything, just stared at each other, eyes beetling to square off any minute. The trail boss worked his teeth together tight and closed his eyes, as if counting until he had calmed himself. When he opened his eyes, he looked at the farmer and said, "Drive 'em on through, boys!"

Within seconds the air filled with the whoops and shouts of encouragement, and the riverside plain became a seething, boiling mass of dust. The sounds of bellowing beeves filled the air as three thousand head of Texas Longhorn cattle lunged, stumbled, and finally broke into a run, tearing down the man's meager two-strand fence; posts snapped and wire pinged and popped as the cattle drove through it. They ran forward at top speed, urged on by the whooping, whip-cracking, pistol-firing trail crew of eight cowboys—straight at the low, one-room ranch house.

The farmer managed to squeeze off two shots, one each from the double-barrel shotgun blasting straight into the pounding herd—whichever cows felt the brunt of the blasts, their cries of pain were drowned out by the thundering herd. The last sounds the farmer made were screams as he half-turned toward the little sod house. But his cries, too, were cut short, pinched off as thousands of hooves punched his bone-weary body into paste.

Within seconds the little house was overrun. Even the rough, knobbed timbers were rendered into pulp and splinters. The sod-and-wood walls, the meager furnishings, all were drummed into the earth of the Texas plains as the herd passed over. And mashed beneath them, the mother and her two children—gone, nothing recognizable left for a decent burial.

The herd thundered on and the cowboys with it. For two months more they drove the cattle north through the Panhandle, through Oklahoma, and on into Kansas, before finally reaching Abilene and the railhead.

They'd been fortunate—other than the dustup with the farmer back on the Neches, the herd hadn't been worked hard and were still nearly as fat and happy as when they'd begun, having worked their way north and into decent grazing land as they hazed them northward.

The men went on a righteous toot in Abilene, painted that town red, black, and blue. They stayed for a month, most of the men blowing the better part of their hard-earned wad on dance-hall floozies hired by the saloon proprietors to do that very task, on watery liquor, and on games of chance that all too often left them dazed, penniless, and out on their ear, weaving on their feet in the dusty street.

And through it all, the haggard cowboys blustered and bragged of their foul deed way back, months before at the farm along the Neches, a tale enjoyed by many ranch hands and cowboys. If it made any of them feel bad, it was but a passing feeling, for ranching and driving cattle was their way of making a living wage, their way of life. A sodbuster would not stand, *could not stand* before the might of a herd of beeves, lives of children and women be damned! Such was their barroom bravado in Abilene that month.

After a fashion, they trailed singly or by twos and threes back out of Kansas, through Oklahoma, and on into Texas, back to their home range where they would winter and work to fill up their coin purses. And as they traveled southward, broke, sober, sore, and malnourished, they began to realize the vicious truth of what they had so recently bragged about. Some of the men avoided the stretch of the Neches where they knew the trampled remains of the sodbuster's place to be. But none of them could have predicted what horrors awaited them as they descended into Texas—and a living hell.

Once back in their home state, each of the eight foot-loose cowboys slowly succumbed to devilish visions of spectral stampeding longhorns and the crushed bodies of the dead family. One by one, they were unable to hold on to their jobs, their sanity, then their very lives. The first to go claimed his life with his own pistol. Another provoked the wrong person in a drunken rage and ended up gutshot in the street. Still another downed cheap whiskey as if drinking were a competitive sport, then expired from its rotting effects, while one of the bedeviled drovers simply stopped eating and soon died of starvation.

The trail boss, the very man who owned the cattle and who had ordered his men to stampede through the farmer's life, was found dead of inexplicable causes along the bank of the Neches, not far from where the splintered remnants of the farmhouse lay. The only sign of something amiss was the look of terror on his face. Within five years, by late 1875, the last of the eight cowboys on the trail drive died. And that's when the hauntings began.

That's when what have come to be known as the Ghost Riders began to appear in the sky over the Neches River. They come in low over the horizon as the sun begins surrendering to the day. The landscape is bathed in a bleeding orange-red glow that illuminates the river's serpentine surface as if it's running red with blood.

The very earth rumbles beneath the feet and anyone unlucky enough to be close by can't help but look skyward in fear. Gouts of great bulky clouds gather, coursing northward even as they re-form and take the shape of a massive, roiling herd of fiery cattle. They have appeared at least once each summer, in the same spot, since 1875, driven on by the doomed souls of those evil-intentioned cowboys all those years ago.

The cowboys' faces are masked behind bandannas, their steeds and the cattle wild-eyed as they tear northward on a drive that will never end. They are doomed to repeat the horrific deeds of their worst moments on earth. And sometimes one of the hellish riders will look groundward and level his fiery gaze on a soul in peril. He will utter an oath of warning to mend one's ways or be doomed to thunder the skies for all eternity with the herd of spectral, devilish cattle as a ghost rider.

In addition to inspiring the famous song "Ghost Riders in the Sky," this legend has legs—a whole herd of them—and can be experienced along the Rio Nueces (aka the Neches

River), which flows from northwest of San Antonio, in Real County, to Lake Corpus Christi down in Live Oak County. It's a fascinating region that seems a likely locale for all manner of dusty ghosts, given the preponderance of hidden canyons and sudden ruins of homes long-ago left to wither in the hot Texas sun, places where the settlers gave up the ghost and left—or stayed and became spirits themselves.

Sometime in the early 1880s, a trail boss had decided to rest his herd and men for the night on a grassy bluff overlooking Blanco Canyon along the eastern edge of the Texas Panhandle. But he hadn't counted on a nester having established himself and his scant forty-head herd, declaring the spot for himself.

"I tell you what, nester," said the boss. "My herd is 1,500 head. I believe we'll be coming on in. It's been a long day and I ain't in no mood to tangle with the likes of you."

The old, broken-down nester let loose with a brown stream of tobacco, dragged a mangy sleeve across his whiskered face, and cocked his rifle. "An' I tell you I ain't about to let you come on in here, ruin a good thing I got going, and mingle my herd with yourn."

The trail boss looked over his shoulder at a couple of his trail hands. "And I tell you, we're coming on through. We'll sort it all out tomorrow. Shouldn't be too difficult, from the looks of your herd." The boss turned his horse back toward his cattle, and within minutes the big herd moved onto the grassy span and set to work grazing.

The old man shouted a few obscenities and shook his fist at every one of the new men, but there was little he could do and he knew it. But he had himself a plan.

Two wranglers were riding watch hours later in the dead of night. Thankfully, the old man hadn't been heard from. And then, without warning, he burst from the brush astride his mule and began whooping and hollering and waving his rain slicker. In no time, he had the herd frenzied and headed toward the high side of the mesa.

The other men heard the commotion, grabbed nearby horses, and rode to turn the herd before inevitable doom occurred. Though they worked like demons, they were able to prevent only half the herd from running straight off the two hundred–foot drop-off. When the morning light came a few hours later, the trail boss took another head count and verified what they already knew: In addition to half the herd, one of the men was missing.

They found Tibbets later, in the pile of dead or writhing, near-dead cattle at the bottom of the cliff. He and his horse had been swept along by the frenzied beasts and driven over the edge while trying to turn them.

The old nester was nowhere to be found. But the trail boss said, "Find him, you, Timms, and Gully. Find him and bring him back. He'll pay for this."

And within hours they brought back the snarling old man, trussed up on his mule like a turkey and howling like a coyote.

"Should we hang him, boss?" one of the men asked.

"Nah, too good for him." The boss rummaged in the blubbering old man's saddlebags and pulled out a filthy shirt. He ripped it in two and handed the pieces to a couple of his cowboys. "Blindfold him and his mule."

The old man set to blubbering harder, alternately howling in anger and fear, writhing and jerking his arms in a vain effort to free his tied arms and legs, but he was bound fast to his saddle. Soon the task was complete.

"You got any words to say, you best get to it."

The old man's lower lip quivered, and he swallowed a couple of times, then said, "What're you fixin' to do to me?"

"Nothing you ain't earned. Now get to praying. We got a man to bury and work to do."

The old man's jaw clenched tight, the muscles in his neck stringing and bulging as he began shouting at them all over again. The trail boss cocked his sidearm, set it on the mule's rump, and fired. The beast lurched forward from the smarting pain of the powder burn and ran straight for the drop-off. The old man screamed the entire time. Soon enough, when he reached the bottom, his screaming stopped abruptly.

"We going to yarn him out of there and bury him?"

"Hell no," said the boss. "He's buzzard bait. But let's give Tibbets a proper burial yonder under that cottonwood."

Despite the gruesome episode, it didn't take long before other herds once again made their way to Stampede Mesa, the name by which it came to be known thereafter. But the cowboys found their relied-upon holding ground had somehow changed. Cowboys who watched the herd at night would see mysterious white cattle emerge from the undergrowth and mingle with their herd. When the cowboys gave chase to the freakish beasts, they found them to be nothing more than cattle-shaped clouds of smoke radiating cold and hell-bent on instigating stampedes. And always the ghost cattle emerged from the east side and were driven toward the high bluffs . . . driven forward by spectral cowboys whooping hard atop ghost horses.

Unfortunately, it took the loss of several herds before trail bosses realized this once-favored holding ground and its spectral ghost herd were best left alone. Even today, more than a century later, the place induces feelings of gloom and vertigo among visitors.

Chapter 26
La Llorona
(The Weeping Woman)

Santa Fe River
Santa Fe, New Mexico & Beyond

La Llorona, Spanish for the "Weeping Woman," is a tall, thin spirit seen and heard along the Santa Fe River. In life she was blessed with beauty and long, flowing black hair—and murderous ways. In a fit of anger, she drowned her two children. Then, in deep remorse, she roamed the Santa Fe River,, wailing and screaming long into the night until she, too, perished. It is said that her angry spirit now searches for children to drag into the water.

"'If only you did not have children'—this is what he told me." The pretty young woman bent low and hissed the words, spittle flecking the faces of the two young boys who huddled together on the rope bed in the corner of the small adobe hut.

The older of the boys shook with fear and hugged his crying little brother tighter. "Mama, I'm sorry, Mama. We'll be good, we'll be good."

This seemed only to spur the woman into a deeper rage. She snatched at the boys' ragged shirtfronts and yanked them off the bed. As she dragged the screaming, thrashing boys out the door, she continued ranting, "I thought he would ask me to marry him tonight. Tonight! How did he find out about you two . . . *diablos?*"

She had returned to the humble home only moments before, early from another night with Señor Nunez. And she had been mad, as mad as the boys had ever seen her. The older boy had been telling his little brother a story about a pretty white horse with a long black mane that ran free over the far mountains, all the way to the place where the dusty earth turned to green, grassy hills. And then their mother came home, and she was angry again. But worse this time.

And now, no matter how hard they struggled, no matter how they screamed, she would not listen. She was so angry, but she was their mama. She had been angry before and she always stopped, maybe after hitting them, making them cry a little, sometimes not letting them eat for a day or two. But that was not so bad, once you got used to it. The older boy knew this, but his little brother was still a baby; he always cried.

Sometimes when their mama was away at night the old lady next door, Mrs. Garza, would sneak over very quietly and give them tortillas, but she would always whisper and tell them never to tell their mama, for she would become angry if she found out.

One night the older boy had asked Mrs. Garza why his mama would be angry about this; the old woman had begun crying and said that it was pride, and vanity. The boy knew nothing about those things, but if that's what made his mama act the way she did, then he did not like pride and vanity. He wondered if they were the names of some of the men Mama was always talking about.

But tonight, tonight she was dragging the two boys out back toward the river, down the bank to the water.

"Mama! No, what are you doing?" She was still in her pretty long dress, the white one that she said made her look good for the men. But he hated that dress because it meant she was going out, and she went out a lot, and always wore that dress. And always she kept it clean. It was a pretty dress, yes, but he hated it. And now this made no sense, for now she was up to her knees in the swift brown water. It was dark but the moon shone off the shiny surface of the river.

Still, Mama wouldn't let go. He looked up at her face, tried to say something more but she pushed him into the water, under the water, and held him down there, grunting. He tried to grab at her arms, her hands, but she was so strong. Beside him, he saw his little brother's face, eyes wide, his little mouth working like a fish, only they weren't fish, they were boys, and they were underwater. He felt funny, like he was warm all over, and he thought that if they were slippery like fish they would be able to swim away from her hands. But still he felt her hand gripping his shirt front.

And the last thing he saw was his mama's face above the water, but she looked all wobbly and angry still. Her mouth was shouting and her long, pretty hair hung half in her face; it even touched the water, and the long white sleeves of the dress were underwater, too. He didn't know what she was shouting, couldn't hear her, but her mouth was moving just like when she was angry.

He tried to look at his little brother, but he couldn't turn his head that way. He knew he was right beside him, though. He thought he felt their heads bump together like Mama did to them sometimes when she was angry with them for not cleaning the house. He wished he was a fish.

Maria stood in the middle of the river, water running down her outstretched arms, her once-white dress now a sodden thing that clung to her long, lean body. But there was nothing attractive about her now. She stood in the new moonlight shuddering and shivering, beginning to wonder what in her rage she had done. It wasn't until she saw the lifeless forms of her boys spinning slowly away from her in the current of the Santa Fe River that she realized what had been done.

It cannot be, she thought. And yet there they were, her boys, floating dead in the water. Stifling sobs, hope welling in her breast, she pushed out into the deepening water and managed to grab hold of the boys, the same shirts she had held so tightly moments before. And as she dragged them to the muddy riverbank, the awful truth dropped her to her knees beside them.

She lifted their thin, limp bodies, tried to force the water from their mouths, pushed their eyelids up, tried to get a response from their glazed, limpid eyes. Even in the moonlight she could see their little lips turning blue; the cold river had robbed them of their warmth.

The foul river. She dragged them farther up the bank and left them there, her mind overwhelmed with the horrible truth of what had been done. Of what that monster woman had done. And then she realized that it was she who had done this thing.

Her wailing roused the nearest neighbors, some distance away along the riverbank. Though they were used to hearing the pretty young woman rage and shriek cruel curses and oaths directed at her two poor children, they had never before heard her so uncontrolled. The screams sounded as if she were being attacked.

When they drew closer, the moonlight shone down on the woman, Maria, so pretty but at the same time something about her frightened them. Other people began arriving, cautiously walking toward her. She didn't appear to see them,

but walked in circles, waving toward the riverbank at something there, bunched on the shore, pointing, letting her arms
drop, throwing back her head and howling like a wild animal.

"*Madre Dios,*" said an old man who held his wife's elbow.
"This is not good. There is something wrong here. Very
wrong and very bad. She is like the devil."

All too soon they realized that the boys were dead.
Whether the young woman killed her own children or whether
the boys had wandered down there on their own, the neighbors did not know. They were aware only that Maria was dis-
tressed. That she could have done this herself didn't make
sense, for what sort of a mother would do such a thing? They
tried to approach her, to calm her, but she was unapproach-
able, untouchable, and lost in her shrieking grief.

As the days passed and the locals buried the boys and
held services, their mother grew more distant, and gripped
by a deep madness. She wandered the riverside, her once-
luminous white dress now mud-spattered, torn, and dragging, her once-shiny black hair now dull and lifeless, and
her tall, thin frame more gaunt by the day as she refused
to eat. There eventually came the day when her corpse was
found floating in the river.

Any thought the locals had of their lives returning to
normal vanished when one night barely a few weeks later,
the people up and down the river for miles began hearing a
howling, crying sound, drawn out and echoing.

And they bore horrified witness to a startling rebirth. It
was then that she gained the name La Llorona, or Weeping
Woman, though she was little more than a ghost, an angry
specter cursing the fates for her most murderous and unforgivable deed, this woman who had been considered among
the prettiest to ever have lived in all the region.

She roamed the riverbanks in a long, flowing white dress looking as if she had not died, and yet had never lived. For she did not walk but seemed to float above the earth, approaching with an unnerving speed and a devilish glint in her eyes anyone who came near her. And she reserved a special anger for children who ventured too close to the water's edge.

It is said that she walks among us still and has broadened her formidable reach, roaming the riverways, streams, lakes, ponds, and drainage and irrigation ditches throughout New Mexico, Old Mexico, Arizona, Texas—she has even been seen as far north as Montana, roaming the banks of the Yellowstone River, where she followed Hispanic migrant workers. And always, in her rage, she looks for children to drag into the water, perhaps in an effort to make up for the loss of her own children.

As much folktale as it is ghost tale, the story of La Llorona, the Weeping Woman of the Santa Fe River, has been around in one form or another since the time of the Conquistadores in the sixteenth century. But it never fails to induce a shiver and a quick glance up and down the riverside, and for good reason: Numerous people have claimed to see the spectral sinner—and sightings continue to this day. Folks in Santa Fe claim she is very much in residence, and anyone who hears her nighttime wailing and moaning, who sees her long, slim form, her white dress glowing as she glides along the riverside, is convinced of her presence. But it is children who should be especially cautious. They are her weakness, and she comes for them.

Chapter 27

Wolf Girl
of Devil's River

Devil's River
Del Rio, Texas

In the 1800s, along the Devil's River in Texas, a trapper's wife went into labor. The trapper rode to a Mexican village for help but died on the way. The villagers found his wife, also dead, but of the baby, there was no sign, though inside and out of the cabin were the tracks of wolves. Over the ensuing years, people saw a wolf pack with an oddly hunched member. She was captured once and many witnessed her before she escaped. To this day, she is seen, surveying strangers from across the river, misshapen and nursing wolf pups, howling and loping the banks of the river.

The skull-cracking thunder drowned out all sound, including the approaching yowl of wolves. The night was near black, save for the slashes of harsher-than-noonday brilliance as lightning stitched through the raw, clacking branches of the cottonwoods. John Dent kept the river to his left, hugging it, and urged the horse forward, concentrating on getting to the village for help. His poor Mollie. . . . He knew now he never should have brought her out to this wild place, especially so close to giving birth. And now she was having trouble.

She was a tall, thin woman, who'd half-jokingly told him she did not have the hips that would make her good at birthing children. He almost smiled at the thought of her, but no, this was no time to fall to musing. She was back at their little trapper's cabin, giving birth to their firstborn, and he had to make all haste to get help for her. He knew only how to take life, how to skin a carcass, strip a wolf's hide from its meat and bone—not how to bring a life into this world.

Without warning his horse balked, great clouds of breath pluming from its snout and its eyes rolling white. It fought him hard, jerking side to side, low gargling whines of fear boiling up from deep in its chest. He'd only ever seen the beast this bothered once, but it had been wolves then, a pack of them closing in one night more than two months before. But it couldn't be wolves out on a night such as this, vicious wind and rain lashing down, the river filling higher with each second.

And then John Dent, too, felt instant, trembling fear deep in his core. It was the earthy, wet-hair stink of meat-eating animal, close and drawing closer, its breath seeming to cloud in his face. His horse whinnied beyond a scream and lost its footing. Dent felt its powerful muscles work frantically to regain solid footing, but there was none to be had, and within seconds, despite his slashing of the reins and jamming the beast hard in the gut, the horse rolled down the bank of the storm-swollen Devil's River.

Lightning sliced the blue-black night, sizzling the wind-driven rain, and time seemed to slow as John Dent slammed down the muddy riverbank. Just before the horse rolled over him, driving him into the river, he saw in the lightning's flash, far above him on the bank, the stark outline of wolves in a ragged line, staring down at him, jumping back and forth over one another, snarling, baying, angry that they had lost such a rich opportunity to the cruelties of weather.

Just before he died, Dent felt himself being dragged along by the roiling river. And though the flow's voice was in fine, full form that night, he swore he heard above it the howl of wolves, as if mocking him, laughing at him. And then they were gone. John Dent's horse-battered body spun downstream.

"There is the gringo trapper's cabin. Poor man, he and his horse must have fallen in the river, perhaps in the storm days ago. They were both found drowned."

"But he was married, no? We shall have to tell his wife."

"That's why we are here. But let me talk, eh? You are, how shall I say it . . . not so good with the ladies."

Mario scowled. Just because he was still unmarried did not mean he would always be so. But he said nothing, just nodded. As they drew closer to the cabin, they realized something was wrong. The chimney sat silent, no smoke trailing from it, then they saw the door was open, swung inward. The two men exchanged looks of concern. For the fall of the year, this would never do. Perhaps the woman was cleaning the place?

"Jorge?"

"Quiet, Mario. Something is wrong." He nodded at the muddied earth. The clearing surrounding the cabin was pocked with many paw prints.

"Wolves."

They entered the open door of the cabin and their hands cupped their mouths, then covered their noses, and they turned away. Back outside, both men began crossing themselves. *"Madre Dios,"* muttered Mario.

For some minutes, neither of them said anything else, then Jorge said, "We have to bury her."

"*Sí.* But I was told she was with child."

They both looked back in the dim, chilled interior, at the muddy paw prints leading in and out of the cabin. "Not anymore."

Chet turned to his friend, Rowley, owner of a neighboring ranch, and thrust his chin toward the riverbank mud. "I tell you, we're on the trail of lobos, all right. But there's something more."

Rowley leaned low out of his saddle, studied the tracks, then sluiced a brown stream of chew juice. "You tellin' me you believe what them Mexicans said about there being a 'Wolf Girl of Devil River'?"

"I don't see how you can think otherwise, what with them tracks and all." Chet stood up. "That's the track of a kid right there."

"They said it was the baby daughter of that dead trapper and his wife, John and Mollie Dent. But that was near fourteen years ago."

"Which would make it just about right that the shepherd boy seen her not but six months ago."

"You got to be kidding me. You don't buy into that, do you?"

Chet continued as if his friend hadn't spoken. "And don't forget the Indians who claim they've seen her 'round these parts, too."

Rowley nodded slowly but didn't take his eyes from his friend's face. "I guess I don't really care one way or the other. I'm just here to shoot me a lobo or two, stop the damned things from killing off more of the critters I have sunk my hard-earned money into. I ain't ranching to fill the bellies of wolves." Rowley chewed in silence for a few moments, then said, "But there ain't no dang way a girl was raised by wolves. That is the stuff of fancy, them dime novels and such."

Suddenly Chet grew silent and looked over his friend's shoulder. "Yep, could be," he said in a whisper. "But it ain't."

"Wha—?"

"Shhhh!" Chet shushed him with a hard look. Then he jerked his chin across the river. There crouched a creature like neither man had ever seen, half hidden in the brush and watching them. It looked more to them like a girl than a wolf.

Within seconds they both spurred their mounts and gave hard chase. The mysterious animal was fleet of foot, but their horses gave them the advantage of speed. The creature loped across open ground and headed for a rocky knob, then turned to face them, backing slowly up the rough rock.

"Drop a loop over her. Don't let 'er get away!" shouted Chet.

"You spent half as much time helping as you do giving orders, by God, we might be able to capture this she-devil!"

Rowley's rope dropped over the snarling girl's shoulders. She snatched at it with filthy, talon-like fingers, but it tightened around her.

Chet jumped down and approached the girl on foot, one hand holding his horse's reins, the other held out as if he were testing the heat of a campfire's flames. "Easy now, girly. Easy, no need to be afraid, we're here to help you. Take you back to the ranch, let the women sort you out. You look a right mess. We'll get you back to your people soon enough."

He approached to within a few feet of the cowering girl who'd retreated far into a cleft in the rock. The rope tightened about her and she struggled against it, all the while silently keeping her eyes trained on the approaching cowboy.

"Easy now, easy." He drew one step closer and that was all it took: The girl screeched and spat at him, lashing out with her arms, oblivious to the tightening rope.

Neither man could fail to notice that, though she was not yet full grown, she was definitely a *she*. Her hair was long, black, and tangled, and hung in her face. She had dark eyes and white teeth in her sneering, howling mouth. She rushed at Chet again and he backed off. His horse jerked from his hand and trotted away, riled by the ruckus and the musky scent of wolves wafting from the howling creature.

"Dang it, girl! We're trying to help you, but if I have to leg it back home, there will be hell to pay."

The two flustered ranchers finally managed to subdue her with ropes. They walked her back to the ranch, keeping her roped taut between them. During the slow trip back, they heard the unmistakable sounds of many light footsteps from the brush, flanking them the entire way. Night closed in just before they got back to the ranch, and they began to regret ever tangling with the crazy Wolf Girl.

Chet and Rowley's wives immediately wanted to scrub her down and cut her hair, maybe get her into a nice, clean dress. But once the men got her into a back bedroom, and the door barely slammed shut, she hurled herself about the room, ripping at the furnishings, howling unintelligible sounds and yowling guttural screeches until they felt sure she was about to expire. They tried the door once when she fell quiet and were barely able to close it again.

Soon, though, an eerie silence closed about the ranch house, and that's when they heard the most frightening sound of all—the neck-prickling howls of an entire pack of wolves surrounding the house. The Wolf Girl responded in kind, issuing heartbreaking howls of her own from within the back bedroom. The men loaded weapons and the women fired up the woodstove and secured the shutters on the insides of the windows. A splintering crash came to them and at the same time, the howling from without abated. Even before they checked, they knew what had happened—the Wolf Girl had pried apart the nailed-shut shutters, smashed the window, and crawled out and away into the dark night.

In the years that followed, numerous people reported seeing the Wolf Girl of Devil's River throughout the brush country of what is now Del Rio, Texas. But the sightings continued long after the girl's natural lifespan should have ended. Too many years had passed, and the creature the girl had become would at best be an old woman. But raised by wolves?

And yet by the early 1970s, she was still being spotted. Three men took a trip to camp and hunt along the Devil's River. Just before dark, one of the men left their site to gather firewood and happened to look across the river. He saw a thin girl, with long, straggly hair draped about her. She was crouched on the opposite bank, digging at something on the ground. She seemed to be surrounded by a faint aura of light, a dim, unnatural glow.

Trembling, the man made his way carefully back up the path to the campsite. His two friends asked him what was wrong, but all he could do was beckon them to follow him back down the trail to the river. They did as he asked, and saw for themselves the glowing Wolf Girl, hunkered low and roaming the bank. And then she fixed her gaze on them and stared. The men bolted for their camp, threw their gear into their truck, and drove as fast as they could back to civilization.

Others since have also seen her, and they all say the Wolf Girl of Devil's River seems not to have aged in more than a century of roving the arid border country of southwestern Texas.

Chapter 28

Spirits of the Anasazi

Anasazi Cliff Dwellings
Mesa Verde National Park, Colorado

Though the "Ancient Ones," the Anasazi Indians, disappeared in AD 1500, their ghosts still walk among the hundreds of rooms in the ruins of their ancient cliff-side dwellings. One can witness their apparitions throughout the massive complex, though most frequently they are seen on the very floor of the canyon, in the kivas— pit houses. Within each kiva is a hole in the floor known by Indians as an "earth navel," or spirit doorway, connecting the living world with the spirit world. Many visitors to the park claim sightings . . . and more. And not all of it is welcome or friendly.

Could it be possible that disturbing the eternal resting place of the dead brings with it an inherent evil, a taint that rises when a grave is exhumed? A stain that feels to the violator of the grave as if it will never wash away? If one were to ask that question of Laura Kingman, she would nod her head and sigh. For she disturbed the grave of an Ancient One.

Half a million people annually visit the 52,074-acre Mesa Verde National Park and its famous cliff dwellings, once home to the mysteriously vanished Anasazi people. And as with many of those visitors, Laura puzzled over how it was that those people from so long ago could carve their snug city into the very cliff walls. And why?

Mesa Verde is, she noted with surprise, a green place, especially after spring rains, where lilies bloom, grasses fur the scape with lush tinges, and insects buzz from plant to plant. She was also shocked to see that vast portions of the mesa itself are burnt, dead trees standing like stark sentries trying to keep intruders at bay.

But Laura was more interested in what the cliff dwellings looked like deep inside. Her tour group visited the mazelike Balcony House, difficult to climb into with its tall ladder and twelve-foot tunnel. But the small group was well rewarded with access to its forty-five rooms and two kivas, pit houses that also contained holes in the floor the Indians referred to as "earth navels," through which, the guide said, spirits passed back and forth from the living world to the dead.

Well into the tour, Laura managed to stray from the group and slipped into the deepest, darkest depths of the place. She flicked on her flashlight and looked over her shoulder. No one following. She swallowed and inched forward, hoping she wouldn't hit her head on the rock ceiling.

And she kept going, for the rock walls did not narrow, but seemed to lure her deeper, as if beckoning toward the center of the earth. She flashed her light into a small space, perhaps eight feet deep and six feet tall, and with rounded walls, both rough and smooth.

What am I looking for? What am I doing this for? I should not have strayed from the group. I am a normal person, she told herself. *But for some reason, I feel a compulsion to explore here. After all,* she thought, *I am on the trip of a lifetime.* At least that's what she'd told all her friends at the insurance office where she worked in Redondo Beach, California.

Now that she found herself in Mesa Verde, she felt as though an amateur archaeologist were blooming within her. So much so that she was sure she wanted to spend her life studying this strange, vanished race. Laura dropped to her knees—a keepsake, something to remember this brief foray by, that's what she needed. Nothing anyone would question or miss. Just a pinch of gravel and she would hurry back along the impossible corridor to her group; she would rejoin, tag along at the end, and no one would be the wiser. She scrabbled in the near dark, her flashlight beam wagging between her teeth, and her hand crabbed down the rough wall to the gravel-strewn floor. There, a bit of grit. No, it was not enough.

She kept on, circling the room and where the wall met the floor and the gravel became softer, her hand bumped something curved, perhaps two inches long, and lighter than a stone of that size would be. She shone her beam on it and knew she'd found her prize. It looked to her untrained eye like a shard of pottery. Her heart beat faster—the Anasazi were famous for their intricate pottery! She closed her fingers over it and stuffed it in her pocket. And that's when Laura's troubles began.

To her horror, Laura realized that her group had moved on. She retraced the route to the entrance and as she emerged from the doorway and worked her way back down the ladder, she heard a man's voice from the dark above, shouting—and drawing closer.

She hurried past a couple of other tourists, staring straight ahead as she walked, hoping whoever the shouting person was would leave her alone. And it worked—the farther she got from the doorway, the quieter the voice became. She hoped it wasn't a ranger or tour guide, and she really hoped whoever it was didn't know that she'd taken the pottery shard.

Laura caught up with her tour group, relieved to note that no one paid her much attention. They were gathered at one of the many kivas that dotted the floor of the canyon.

The guide explained that each one was of particular impor-
tance. They all gathered in the center of the pit house,
around a hole in the floor, what the guide called a spirit
gateway—the very thought of it made Laura shudder inside.
What would happen if she actually saw a ghost of an Anasazi? She'd heard the mesa might well be haunted.

They were all crowded around the spirit gateway, listening to the tour guide, but Laura didn't hear a word he said.
She had begun to worry about what she'd done. Then, as they
watched, a wisp of what looked like smoke trailed up fast
from the hole, and a strange voice erupted all around them,
almost a screeching. It was as if they were all being berated,
but in no language any of them had ever heard. Some of them
looked to the tour guide, wondering if this was somehow part
of his presentation, but he seemed as startled as they.

The voice, that of an angry old man, continued to rant
and swirl about them. Then it was accompanied by the wispy
shadow-and-smoke vapor that swirled among them, constantly forming, re-forming, and dissipating. It centered on
each of them just behind their heads, as if testing them, before
moving to the next person. As it passed by them, over them,
through them, each person felt a fleeting wave of coldness.

No one quite knew what to do. Even the ranger still
seemed puzzled and looked from face to face at the members
of his group, but no one seemed guilty of playing a trick
such as this.

Then the vaporous smoke and voice settled behind Laura
and became louder, swirled taller—and wouldn't leave her
alone. Her heart pounded, her face turned red, and she
shook all over. Finally she could take it no longer and covered her face and cried. And still the smoke swirled and the
voice harried her, sounding more irate as the seconds wore

on. The other members of the tour group backed away from her and then left the kiva, bolting together for the exit. Laura backed up to the nearest stone wall and hugged herself. Still, the strange voice ranted, from behind her, right through the rock. From each side, from above—it seemed to dart about like a fly.

The guide came up, eyes narrowed, and spoke close to her. "Ma'am, have you . . . do you have something that, perhaps, you found? Something that came from within a chamber here at Mesa Verde?"

She looked at him and saw that he understood. He also saw that he was offering her a way out of this frightening predicament. "I didn't steal."

He nodded, smiling. "You're not the first to have this happen, you know."

"I only wanted something to remember this place by." Laura couldn't meet his gaze.

"I understand. I work here and yet every day I find out something fascinating about it."

She reached into her pants pocket and pulled out the pottery shard. As she held it out in her palm, the voice grew more strident and the mist swirled low over it, covering her hand. Laura resisted the urge to throw the shard.

In the light, it didn't look like much of anything, but she knew it was valuable, at least to the ranting ghost. She tried to hand it to the tour guide, but he shook his head and beckoned her to the doorway. The spirit smoke spun around the pit in the center of the chamber, then disappeared into it, and with it, the shrieking voice, satisfied, it appeared, that Laura would soon return the looted shard to its rightful place.

"Let's go together and put it back," said the guide, talking as they headed back to Balcony House. "Then you can be sure it's been taken care of. You don't want this old spirit to haunt you forever, do you?"

Laura's eyes grew wide. "Would that really happen?"

"Unofficially, I can tell you that this place is full of spirits and some of them aren't so forgiving of their homes being looted. You've met one of the cranky ones. But some are downright foul. I've heard stories of looters' lives changing once they left Mesa Verde. And not in good ways. As far as I'm concerned, it's not worth the risk." He looked at her as they walked. "And it's illegal."

Laura's hopes fell. "You're going to have to report me, aren't you?"

"I'll tell you what. Why don't you buy a memento at the gift shop, or make a donation that will help fund upkeep of the place. Who knows, maybe you'll want to come visit us again next year."

As Laura made the climb back into Balcony House, she wondered if Hawaii had many ghosts.

Mesa Verde National Park is the only US national park devoted to human creations. This fact is especially impressive when one considers the Anasazi ("Ancient Ones" in Navajo), Stone Age people, were able to build these elaborate dwellings without the assistance of metal tools. Of the 4,700 archaeological sites at Mesa Verde, most of its 600 cliff dwellings were built between AD 1230 and 1260. Though the Anasazi inhabited the top of the mesa for more than seven hundred years, it was not until the last seventy-five to one hundred years of their time there that they built their elaborate cliff-side dwellings.

Mesa Verde was abandoned near the end of the thirteenth century, for reasons modern archaeologists assume had to do with successive years of crop failures due to erratic rainfall and ending with a thirty-year drought. It is also speculated that nomadic tribes such as the Utes, Paiutes, and Navajos may have begun to venture northwest at roughly the same time. Ruins of other Anasazi sites can be found throughout the Four Corners region of the Southwest, which includes southwestern Colorado, southern Utah, northwestern New Mexico, and northern Arizona.

While they were in residence at Mesa Verde, the Anasazi were among the more advanced cultures in North America— the 4,700 archaeological sites at Mesa Verde include mesa-top pueblos, reservoirs, towers, and farming terraces. Below the rim, the many impressive cliff dwellings include Balcony House. On a high, east-facing ledge, Balcony House contains forty-five rooms and two kivas, and requires visitors to climb a thirty-two-foot ladder before crawling through a twelve-foot tunnel.

The largest of the dwellings at Mesa Verde National Park is Cliff Palace, the largest cliff dwelling in the world. In addition to 75 open areas, Cliff Palace contains 150 rooms housing roughly 120 people, 25 to 30 of the rooms show signs of being used for residential purposes, and 23 of the rooms are kivas, or rooms built underground for use in religious ceremonies.

Today, when people of Navajo or Zuni descent assist in archaeological digs at these prehistoric sites, they will do so only with the assistance of a charm that helps them escape the certain anger of disrupted ghosts. Despite such precautions, many of these locations, long ago violated for their bones, beads, pottery, and other relics, are in a constant state of spiritual turmoil.

Appendix A
"Wanted" Posters

Though I consulted hundreds of books, pamphlets, periodicals, and websites while writing *Haunted Old West*, I've nibbled that list down to a short stack of resources that should prove helpful and of interest to fans of the haunted and historic Old West.

In addition to the resources listed here, I also recommend visiting local libraries, historical societies, museums, and folklife centers. Not only do they have wonderful, extensive archives filled with all manner of media and ephemera, but they also are staffed with real live people (and the occasional ghost) whose business and passion it is to know about the Old West in its many forms, spiritual or otherwise.

BOOKS

Asfar, Dan. *Ghosts Stories of the Old West*. Edmonton, Canada: Ghost House Books, 2003. This one's a fine collection of some of the historic West's most intriguing paranormal tales.

Belanger, Jeff. *Encyclopedia of Haunted Places*. Edison, NJ: Castle Books, 2008. This useful reference covers the United States, Canada, and elsewhere, and is broken down regionally and peppered with firsthand accounts by ghost hunters.

Dobie, J. Frank. *The Longhorns*. New York: Bramhall House, 1982. This fascinating book tells all about the Longhorn breed, cowboys, cattle drives, stampedes, rustlers, and more.

Donovan, Jim. *Custer and Little Bighorn: The Man, the Mystery, the Myth*. Stillwater, OK: Voyageur Press, 2001. A solid book about one of the most talked-about figures in American history.

Dow, James R., Susan D. Dow, and Roger L. Welsch, eds. *Wyoming Folklore*. Lincoln: University of Nebraska Press, 2010. A fascinating book of folklore and history collected and documented by teachers, writers, and scholars during the Depression as part of the Federal Writers Project (FWP).

Etulain, W. Richard, and Glenda Riley, eds. *With Badges & Bullets: Lawmen & Outlaws in the Old West*. Golden, CO: Fulcrum Publishing, 1999. This book helps put flesh on the rattling bones of some of the most infamous figures of the Old West.

Graham, W. A. *The Story of the Little Big Horn*. Mechanicsburg, PA: Stackpole Books, 1994. One of many books to deal squarely with the battle that won't die.

Guthrie, C. W. *The Pony Express: An Illustrated History*. Guilford, CT: TwoDot/Globe Pequot Press, 2010. This excellent book combines the legends and lore of the famed mail service with photography and documents.

Hauck, Dennis William. *Haunted Places: The National Directory*. New York: Penguin Books, 2002. A most useful reference work organized alphabetically by state, it gives readers more than two thousand entries on sites of paranormal activity.

Horan, James D. *The Authentic Wild West*: Vol. 1, *The Gunfighters*. Vol. 2, *The Outlaws*. New York: Crown Publishers, 1976–1980. Good references that never fail to inform.

Johnson, Dorothy M. *The Bloody Bozeman*. Missoula, MT: Mountain Press Publishing, 1983. An artful book depicting the often-brutal quest for gold in Montana, written by a master.

Knowles, Thomas, and Joe Lansdale, eds. *The West That Was*. New York: Wings Books, 1993. A fun, authoritative story-and-picture album covering the Old West from all angles, by award-winning writers of the West.

Lamar, Howard R., ed. *The New Encyclopedia of the American West*. New Haven, CT: Yale University Press, 1998. One big, useful resource.

Mayo, Matthew P. *Cowboys, Mountain Men & Grizzly Bears: Fifty of the Grittiest Moments in the History of the Wild West*. Helena, MT: TwoDot/Globe Pequot Press, 2009. Just as its title promises, a lively collection of true and gritty tales of the Old West.

———. *Sourdoughs, Claim Jumpers & Dry Gulchers: Fifty of the Grittiest Moments in the History of Frontier Prospecting*. Helena, MT: TwoDot/Globe Pequot Press, 2012. Just as its title promises, a lively collection of true and gritty tales of prospecting in the Old West and far north.

McLynn, Frank. *Wagons West: The Epic Story of America's Overland Trails*. New York: Grove Press, 2002. An unvarnished, well-written book about America's overlanders.

McMurtry, Larry. *Oh What a Slaughter: Massacres in the American West, 1846–1890*. New York: Simon & Schuster, 2005. A fascinating book about man's unending desire to inflict brutality on his fellows.

Murray, Earl. *Ghosts of the Old West*. New York: TOR, 1988. A well-written book presenting all manner of eerie encounters and paranormal activity in the Old West.

Ogden, Tom. *Haunted Cemeteries*. Guilford, CT: Globe Pequot Press, 2010. This one presents twenty-five ghostly tales of paranormal happenings in cemeteries across America and beyond.

———. *Haunted Hotels*. Guilford, CT: Globe Pequot Press, 2010. Covers twenty-five chilling tales of paranormal happenings in hotels, inns, and rooming houses across America and beyond.

Pace, Dick. *Golden Gulch: The Story of Montana's Fabulous Alder Gulch*. Montana: Dick Pace, 1962. A slim book that documents the history of this boom-bust town.

Reed, Robert C. *Train Wrecks: A Pictorial History of Accidents on the Main Line*. New York: Bonanza Books, 1968. Just what its title promises: a fascinating compendium of train wrecks.

Seagraves, Anne. *Soiled Doves: Prostitution in the Early West*. Hayden, ID: Wesanne Publications, 1994. A history of the world's oldest profession as plied in the Old West.

Smith, Barbara. *Ghost Stories of the Rocky Mountains*. Edmonton, Canada: Lone Pine Publishing, 1999. Dozens of spine-tingling stories that prove the Rocky Mountains are among the most haunted landscapes in the world.

Stewart, R. George. *Ordeal by Hunger: The Story of the Donner Party*. Lincoln: University of Nebraska Press, 1986. One of many good books about this tragic episode in American history.

Taylor, Troy. *Out Past the Campfire Light*. Alton, IL: Whitechapel Productions Press, 2004. A fun book filled with accounts of missing people, lost mines, mysterious creatures, eerie spots, and more, from all over the West and beyond.

Vestal, Stanley. *The Old Santa Fe Trail*. Lincoln: University of Nebraska Press, 1996. A fine history of one of the major travel routes of the Old West.

WEBSITES

www.americanfolklore.net

A fun site brimming with myths, legends, fairy tales, superstitions, and ghost stories from all over the United States—and beyond.

www.ghosthaunts.com

A big site filled with all manner of information about ghosts and haunted places.

www.haunted-places.com

The online version of the *Haunted Directory* reference book, a great starting point for finding out more about paranormal activities anywhere.

www.legendsofamerica.com

A huge and useful site stuffed with all manner of historical information, photos, artwork, articles, anecdotal information, and more.

www.prairieghosts.com

A site filled with intriguing information about anything and everything mysterious.

www.theshadowlands.net

Another fascinating and useful site that covers the unexplained and inexplicable.

Appendix B

Saddle Up, Pard!

There's nothing like roving today's West—in search of the *Old* West—to try to catch sight of a spectral Indian or a ghostly cowpoke in the act of scaring the chaps off someone. This list provides basic information (addresses, telephone numbers, websites, directions, and more) that will serve as a handy starting point for anyone eager to ghost hunt on their own in the Wild and Woolly West.

If a certain haunted location is on your must-see list, *always* call ahead and *always* research it thoroughly first. Be aware that change is constant: Properties change ownership, web addresses, phone numbers, and the like become outdated, and ghosts sometimes do move on. Many properties are businesses (e.g., hotels, saloons), others are private, and some might lead you to the middle of nowhere. Be aware of your limitations, prepare accordingly, and above all, be respectful of private property owners, of businesses, of patrons of said businesses, of the natural landscape, of opening and closing times, and of residents of the spirit world, too.

Note: Neither the author nor the publisher is affiliated with any of the locations, services, or businesses mentioned in Haunted Old West. *Their appearance in this listing should not be construed as an endorsement, invitation, recommendation, or advertisement in any way.*

PART ONE: WAGON TRAIL, EXPRESS STATION & TRAIN TRACK

Chapter 1: Dead Man's Canyon
Dead Man's Canyon
Highway 115, near Colorado Springs, Colorado
www.waymarking.com/waymarks/WM8HXC_Henry_
Harkins_Dead_Mans_Canyon_El_Paso_County_CO
Up for a visit to Dead Man's Canyon? Henry Harkins's grave can be found on the southeast side of Highway 115, surrounded by a white picket fence. It was moved there in 1965 to accommodate the new road. The grave site is fifteen miles outside of Colorado Springs, ten miles south of the main entrance to Fort Carson. Headed north, it's ten miles north of Turkey Creek Road.

Chapter 2: Beckoning Wraiths of Cheyenne Pass
Cheyenne Pass
East of Laramie, Wyoming
Head west toward Laramie and you'll drive through the pass. Keep an eye or two peeled for peculiar shapes rising from the landscape to either side of the car as you drive on through. And if they happen to motion toward you, good luck!

Chapter 3: Phantom Workers of Dove Creek Camp
Sinks of Dove Creek
Near Kelton, Utah
(435) 471-2209, ext. 29
www.nps.gov/gosp/index.htm
The Sinks of Dove Creek are located along an old railroad bed near Kelton, Utah. However, the ideal—and interesting—place

to begin this foray is at the Golden Spike National Historic Site, thirty-two miles west of Brigham City, on Highway 83 near Promontory Point.

Chapter 4: Ghost Rider of the Pony Express

Hollenberg Station State Historic Site
2889 23rd Rd.
Hanover, Kansas
(785) 337-2635
www.kshs.org/portal_hollenberg
Hollenberg Station is the only Pony Express station that still stands in its unaltered state on its original site. Nearby, a visitor center complete with interpretive exhibits has been built.

Fort Leavenworth
Leavenworth, Kansas
(913) 684-3186
www.kansastravel.org/fortleavenworth.htm
Visits to the National Cemetery and the Frontier Army Museum are recommended.

Chapter 5: Tragic Spirits of the Donner Party

Donner Memorial State Park
Truckee, California
(530) 582-7892
www.parks.ca.gov/?page_id=503
This handsome park lies one hundred miles east of Sacramento on Interstate 80, within the town of Truckee, west of downtown on the south side of the freeway. Of special interest are the various memorials to the Donner Party.

Chapter 6: Bandit Ghoul of Six Mile Canyon
Six Mile Canyon
Off Highway 341, east of Virginia City, Nevada
www.visitvirginiacitynv.com
From the east on Highway 50, take a right onto the unpaved eleven-mile stretch of Six Mile Canyon Road. Gold was first discovered at the head of the canyon in 1859, and it's still found throughout the region today. And the loot buried by Big Jack Davis? Apparently it's still out there. . . .

PART TWO: MINE CAMP, BOOM TOWN & GRAVEYARD
Chapter 7: Ghoulish Garnet
Ghost Town of Garnet
Garnet, Montana
Bureau of Land Management
(406) 329-3914
garnetghosttown@gmail.com
www.garnetghosttown.net
From Montana Route 200, turn south at the Garnet Range Road between mile markers 22 and 23, thirty miles east of Missoula. Follow the Range Road twelve miles to Garnet's parking area. Though Montana's best-preserved ghost town is open year-round, wheeled vehicles are allowed on the road only from May to January.

Chapter 8: Tommyknockers of the Mamie R. Mine
Raven Hill
Cripple Creek, Colorado
(877) 858-4653
www.cripple-creek.co.us
Since the location of the Mamie R. Mine is lost to history (official census data on mine locations began to be collected the year after the mine closed in 1894), the next best thing is for the curious to pay a visit to Cripple Creek, Colorado, a bustling town with a long, rich mining history.

Chapter 9: Sinkpit of Sin and Damnation
Ghost Town of Bodie, State Historic Park
Bodie, California
(760) 647-6445
www.bodie.com
www.bodiehistory.com
www.parks.ca.gov/?page_id=509
The Bodie State Historic Park is located northeast of Yosemite, thirteen miles east of Highway 395 on Bodie Road (Highway 270), seven miles south of Bridgeport. From US 395, take State Route 270. Head east for ten miles until the pavement ends, then continue for three miles on a dirt road to Bodie. The park is closed during periods of inclement weather. Calling ahead is strongly recommended.

Chapter 10: Boot Hill and Beyond
Boot Hill Cemetery
Idaho City, Idaho
(208) 392-4159
www.idahocitychamber.com
www.diamondlils.net
Idaho City is located forty-five minutes northeast of Boise and can be found by following State Highway 21. Once there, Boot Hill Cemetery can be found just northeast of town, and Pioneer Cemetery isn't far, on—you guessed it—Cemetery Road. But what's your hurry? Stop in for a bite and a brew at Diamond Lil's Steakhouse and Saloon, and wander this history-rich gold-rush town.

Chapter 11: Oregon's Forbidden Ground
The Oregon Vortex
4303 Left Fork Sardine Creek Rd.
Gold Hill, Oregon
(541) 855-1543
www.oregonvortex.com
mystery@oregonvortex.com
Well worth the visit—if you can stand to have your visual and mental perceptions challenged! The Oregon Vortex is located just outside the rural town of Gold Hill, halfway between the cities of Grants Pass and Medford, in the beautiful Rogue River Valley.

PART THREE: HOTEL, BROTHEL & SALOON
Chapter 12: Hauntings at the Hot Springs
Chico Hot Springs Resort & Day Spa
1 Old Chico Rd.
Pray, Montana
(800) 468-9232
www.chicohotsprings.com
From Highway 89, turn at the flashing yellow light at Emigrant, drive 1.2 miles to the stop sign, turn left and travel 0.5 miles to the Chico road, then turn right. Chico Hot Springs is another 1.6 miles at the end of the paved road. Then it's soak, dine, and wine . . . but don't forget to ask about the ghosts!

Chapter 13: The Swamper
Big Nose Kate's Saloon
417 E. Allen St.
Tombstone, Arizona
(520) 457-3107
www.bignosekates.info
www.cityoftombstone.com
Big Nose Kate's Saloon is a National Historic Landmark that serves all manner of tasty food, beverages, and is smack-dab in a city that typifies Old West history. Must-see sites are too numerous to mention, but you can't go wrong in spending a whole lot of time in and around Tombstone.

Chapter 14: Ghost Host of the Bullock
The Historic Bullock Hotel
633 Main St.
Deadwood, South Dakota
(800) 336-1876
www.historicbullock.com
Considered one of the finest hotels in all the Old West, the Bullock still earns that claim. Walking in the front door is like stepping back in time. The Bullock offers an on-site casino, a saloon, and fine dining—oh, and the kindly if attentive ghost of one of the Old West's most famous town tamers.

Chapter 15: The Longest Night . . . Ever
The Phantom Saloon
Park County, Wyoming
To visit the Phantom Saloon of Park County, Wyoming, simply become lost in a blizzard and ride your horse until death nearly claims you, then find the little shack that shouldn't be there—and as you shakily kindle a fire in the fireplace, be sure to keep one eye aimed behind you.

Chapter 16: The Bloody St. James
St. James Hotel
617 S. Collison Ave.
Cimarron, New Mexico
(888) 376-2664
events@exstjames.com
www.exstjames.com
The St. James, no longer as "bloody" as it once was, has nonetheless been welcoming guests for well over a century. Accommodation can be made in the original historic (and

haunted!) rooms, surrounded by nineteenth-century splendor, or the newer (unhaunted!) two-story attached annex.

Chapter 17: Ghost Bride of the Golden North
Golden North Hotel
Corner of Third and Broadway
Skagway, Alaska
While the hotel hasn't offered accommodation since 2002, the ground floor has been turned into shops for the tourist traffic, primarily from cruise ships in the summer. It is believed that the ghosts still inhabit their rooms, perhaps waiting for the day when the hotel once again opens its doors to (living) overnight guests.

PART FOUR: PRISON, FORT & BATTLEFIELD
Chapter 18: The Unliving Hell of Yuma Prison
Yuma Territorial Prison State Historic Park
1 Prison Hill Rd.
Yuma, Arizona
(928) 783-4771
www.azstateparks.com/parks/YUTE
A visit to Yuma Territorial Prison is often an unforgettable experience. Just peering into the dark stone cells evokes the gritty history of Old West justice. Throughout the year, groups of reenactors help bring the place alive once again. No one knows how the ghosts feel about this.

Hotel Lee
390 S. Main St.
Yuma, Arizona
(928) 783-9614
www.hotellee.com
In the nearby town of Yuma, the haunted Hotel Lee is home
to a number of spirits who would love to make you feel at
ease. . . .

Chapter 19: Restless at Reno Crossing
Little Bighorn Battlefield National Monument
Crow Agency, Montana
(406) 638-3214
www.nps.gov/libi/index.htm
To get to this impressive 765.34-acre historic site from Interstate 90, take exit 510, Highway 212. The site was established as a National Monument on March 22, 1946, and is,
above all else, a cemetery that should be treated with the
utmost care and respect.

Chapter 20: Spirits of the Alamo
The Alamo
300 Alamo Plaza
San Antonio, Texas
(210) 255-1391
www.thealamo.org
Be one of the millions of people each year to visit the historic 4.2-acre compound. Although the Alamo officially fell
to the might of the Mexican army's numbers on the morning
of March 6, 1836, the place is alive with history—and as one
of the most haunted spots in the United States, it's home to
an incredible number of ghosts.

Chapter 21: Haunted Warbonnet Creek

Warbonnet Battlefield Monument

Sioux County, Northwestern Nebraska

From Hot Springs, South Dakota, take Highway 71 south to the intersection of Toadstool Road, then travel thirty-seven miles to Hat Creek Road, then one mile south to Montrose, then nine miles to the Warbonnet Battlefield Monument, which is sited atop a steep hill. The site is open year-round and is frequented by reenactment groups who routinely experience paranormal activity.

PART FIVE: RANCH, MANSION & MARKET

Chapter 22: Ghostly Guilt of the Winchester Heir

Winchester Mystery House

525 S. Winchester Blvd.

San Jose, California

(408) 247-2101

www.winchestermysteryhouse.com

This amazing complex is so impressive and odd that it should be on everyone's to-visit list, ghost hunter or nonbeliever (though tours tend to make believers out of even the staunchest skeptics). Guided tours are offered of the house that has 160 rooms, 47 fireplaces, 17 chimneys, 2 ballrooms, numerous ghosts . . . you get the idea.

Chapter 23: Prairie Parties at 101 Ranch

The Miller Brothers' 101 Ranch
101 Ranch Memorial Rd. (State Highway 156)
Kay County, Oklahoma
www.101ranchota.com
www.kaycounty.info/101_ranch
In 1990 the Oklahoma Legislature designated State Highway 156 as the 101 Ranch Memorial Road. An historical marker is located on the highway about thirteen miles southwest of Ponca City. The 101 Ranch site is open to the public, but caretakers ask that it be treated with respect.

Chapter 24: Pike Place Ghosts

Pike Place Market
85 Pike St.
Seattle, Washington
(206) 682-7453
www.pikeplacemarket.org
Sure, you could stand around and hope to see a ghost or two—and well you might—but why not browse the shops, grab a meal or fresh produce, and take in a street performance at America's biggest farmers' market (and more) on nine acres. Plenty to do before the nighttime ghosts come out to play. And then the real fun begins!

Market Ghost Tour
1410 Post Alley
Seattle, Washington
www.marketghost.com
If you're not sure where to begin your quest, try one of
several ghost-centric tours, guaranteed to thrill and chill.
Don't forget to bring some ABC (Already Been Chewed) gum
for the Gum Wall.

PART SIX: COWBOY, INDIAN & BEAST
Chapter 25: Neches River Hell Riders
The Neches River
Northwest of San Antonio, Texas
On hot summer afternoons in Texas, along the Rio Nueces
(aka the Neches River, which flows from northwest of San
Antonio, in Real County, to Lake Corpus Christi down in Live
Oak County), keep an eye out for peculiar masses of rolling
clouds that suddenly act as if they're being whipped into a
frenzy. They are. Before long they'll form into huge, ghostly
shapes of cattle driven by demon wranglers.

Stampede Mesa
In Crosby County, where the eastern edge of the Panhandle
hits the Red River, just east and south sits Blanco Canyon
Reservoir. On the east side of the lake, a peninsula of land
juts into the lake. That's the spot. It's been called one of the
most haunted locales in all of Texas—and given the size of
the Lone Star State, that's saying something.

Chapter 26: *La Llorona* (The Weeping Woman)

Santa Fe River

Santa Fe, New Mexico & Beyond

www.santafenm.gov

www.santafe.org

While in this historic Old West town, soak up the South-western ambience, sample the tasty cuisine, and stroll the banks of the Santa Fe River and listen for the wailing of La Llorona. But keep a tight grip on the kids, lest she try to pull them in!

Historic Walks of Santa Fe

(505) 986-8388

www.historicwalksofsantafe.com

One of the best ways to see all that this amazing city has to offer—highly recommended.

Chapter 27: Wolf Girl of Devil's River

Devil's River

Del Rio, Texas

In the southwest desert country of Texas, near Del Rio, runs the Devil's River. Along the scrub country where javelina squeal, snakes slither, and the unforgiving sun bleaches everything below, the phantom Wolf Girl of Devil's River can still be spied suckling pups, howling at the night sky, and roving the riverbanks. She has passed from rumor to legend to ghostly myth in southwest Texas. No one knows whether she is more afraid of you or if you will be of her. That's up to you to find out.

Chapter 28: Spirits of the Anasazi
Anasazi Cliff Dwellings
Mesa Verde National Park, Colorado
(970) 529-4465
www.nps.gov/meve/index.htm
The park is a one-hour drive from Cortez, Colorado, east
on Highway 160. From Durango, Colorado, heading west on
Highway 160, the park is a 1.5-hour drive. The cliff dwellings at Mesa Verde are incredible and should not be missed.
But don't forget to visit Park Point, the highest elevation in
the park at 8,427 feet, and take in the stunning 360-degree
views of the surrounding landscape. The Anasazi inhabited
one of the prettiest places in the world. Maybe that's why
they refuse to leave. . . .

About the Author

Matthew P. Mayo's short stories have appeared in a variety of publications, including *Beat to a Pulp*, *Out of the Gutter*, Moonstone Books anthologies, and the DAW Books anthologies *Timeshares* and *Steampunk'd*. His story "Half a Pig," from the anthology *A Fistful of Legends*, was selected as a 2010 Spur Award Finalist by the Western Writers of America. His story "Scourge of the Spoils," from the DAW anthology *Steampunk'd*, was selected as a 2010 Peacemaker Award Finalist by Western Fictioneers.

Matthew's novels include the westerns *Winters' War*; *Wrong Town*; *Hot Lead, Cold Heart*; and *Dead Man's Ranch*. His critically acclaimed nonfiction books include *Cowboys, Mountain Men & Grizzly Bears: Fifty of the Grittiest Moments in the History of the Wild West*; *Bootleggers, Lobstermen & Lumberjacks: Fifty of the Grittiest Moments in the History of Hardscrabble New England*; and *Sourdoughs, Claim Jumpers & Dry Gulchers: Fifty of the Grittiest Moments in the History of Frontier Prospecting*.

He has also written, in collaboration with his wife, photographer Jennifer Smith-Mayo, the coffee-table books *Maine Icons*, *New Hampshire Icons*, and *Vermont Icons*. Matthew haunts the coast of Maine with his wife and dog, where they prowl for the unexplained and unexpected. Visit him on the web at www.matthewmayo.com. And bring an EMF meter!